HIS FROST MAIDEN

SPACE LORDS: A QURILIXEN WORLD NOVEL

MICHELLE M. PILLOW

MICHELLE M. PILLOW® - MICHELLEPILLOW.COM

His Frost Maiden (Space Lords) © Copyright 2007 - 2018, Michelle M. Pillow

Cover art © Copyright 2014

Originally Published as: Frost Maiden

Fourth Printing July 2018, The Raven Books LLC

Third Electronic Printing October 2014

Second Electronic Printing April 2011

First Electronic Printing December 2007

ISBN 978-1-62501-196-1

Published by The Raven Books LLC

To J.R.A.
Faafetai.
Thank you for the dynamic conversations, language and anthropological lessons, and general feeding of the creative madness. As you begin your journeys across the world, through unseen dimensions and a universe of imagination, try to stay a little bit grounded in reality... but not too grounded. Living in complete reality is overrated.
Good luck in whichever dimension you settle in, and consider me a friend in all.

SPACE LORDS SERIES

His Frost Maiden
His Fire Maiden
His Metal Maiden
His Earth Maiden
His Woodland Maiden

ABOUT HIS FROST MAIDEN

A Dragon Lords World Romance

Empath and space pirate, Evan Cormier is obsessed with decoding an ominous premonition about his future. When a fellow crewman angered a spirit, the vengeful Zhang An took her wrath out on everyone in the vicinity. Evan just happened to be one of them. He's now facing a future in which he'll be forever alone.

Lady Josselyn of the House of Craven has been betrayed. With her home world on a Florencian moon under attack and her family dead, she finds herself at the mercy of the one who deceived them. There is only one thing left to do—die with honor. But before she can join her family in the afterlife, she must first avenge all that she held dear. Falling in love with a pirate was never in the plan. Evan and his thieving crewmates might have delayed her fate, but they can't stop destiny.

Space Lords is a continuation of the bestselling Dragon Lords series and Lords of the Var® *series.*

Qurilixen World Novels

Dragon Lords Series

Barbarian Prince

Perfect Prince

Dark Prince

Warrior Prince

His Highness The Duke

The Stubborn Lord

The Reluctant Lord

The Impatient Lord

The Dragon's Queen

Dynasty Lords Series
Seduction of the Phoenix
Temptation of the Butterfly

To learn more about the Qurilixen World series of
books and to stay up to date on the latest book list
visit www.MichellePillow.com

AUTHOR UPDATES

To stay informed about when a new book in the
series installments is released, sign up for updates:

http://michellepillow.com/author-updates/

NOTE FROM THE AUTHOR

Dear Readers,

I'm pleased to present you with the next install-ment of my ongoing Dragon Lords World stories, the series: Space Lords. These books continue the Bestselling Dragon Lords, *Lords of the Var*®, and Zhang Dynasty series. For those of you catching up on the series, a complete reading order list is avail-able on my website, www.michellepillow.com.

Though they can be read alone, I recommend reading books in order of release for optimal enjoy-ment. For details please visit me on the web at www.michellepillow.com. Thank you for your continual support of this project and your wonderful emails.

Happy Reading!
Michelle

CHAPTER 1

PROLOGUE: CRAVEN ESTATES, EARTH SETTLEMENT, FLORENCIA'S FIFTH MOON

"Josselyn Craven, you stand accused of crimes against the human race. Your title, family property, and your wealth are hereby stripped."

The intricate patterns of the old woven carpet came into focus under Josselyn's face. Though each curve was as familiar to her as the bricks of her home, she had never seen them so close. Nor had she seen the sticky crimson stain now marring the once rich texture. Her hand shaking, she ran it by her face, knowing before she looked that it was blood. The acrid smell was all too potent as it curled into her nostrils. There was too much of it to be her blood. But whose? A servant? Were they all to be slaughtered?

Sacrelue!

444

Her muscles ached from the hours spent running around her large castle home, fighting off her attackers. She'd lost her sword below in the corridor by the main hall and now had no weaponry—not that she had the energy to lift much beyond her own weight. Josselyn's father had seen to it she was trained as well as any man, but she couldn't fight off the endless stream of soldiers that seemed to fill the halls. Sneaking through secret passages—those hidden behind the stone walls— she'd made her way from her bedchamber only to nearly escape through a high window. Her sides were scraped from the tight fit, but the ache was dull compared to the sharp stab of her broken ribs, the burning pull of a dislocated shoulder, and the myriad of bruises. All injuries were left by her Florencia Moon Coalition peers turned Federation lackeys. How some of the men looked like they enjoyed hitting her, watching as the last of the mighty Craven family fell.

Though they claimed it was the Florencian government, the so-called rebels knew the truth. The Federation was behind the new policies ruining their freedom and their lives. Like the classic Old Earth tale of the nobleman who hid his true nature in order to save his people from a corrupt government, so too had her family hid in the limelight of society.

Now, for their troubles, there were only three Cravens left. She'd seen her father fall, her three older brothers, too. The oldest, Jonathan, to a sword, the next in line, Peter, to an axe, and Ralphe to a dagger. Their dead bodies were strewn all over the castle, their blood staining the floors, marring her gown from where she'd held them. Hopefully one brother, the one whose body she had yet to find, had escaped. Rainier was the youngest at ten and two years, but resourceful. Then there was her mother, Lady Craven, who thankfully was off planet. At least she was safe. Lady Craven was not a fighter. She was a good, gentle woman with a heart big enough for the whole galaxy. The lady was protected by her family from most of their rebellious affairs.

If only Rainier had gone with Lady Craven, as had been the original plan, then Josselyn wouldn't have to worry about the boy's safety. Even as she thought it, she knew the most likely scenario was that Rainier lay on a bloody, stone deathbed. The idea of him, alone and dying, tore at her. Even this blood stained carpet beneath her could have been his resting place.

Shaking, she pushed up, her heart aching with the carnage she'd seen. Grief overwhelmed her spirit, even as it drove her body angrily on. She didn't think on tomorrow, to the time when she'd have to face what had happened. It was all gone. Her life. Destroyed. Empty.

It's only a matter of time before they kill the rest, her mind whispered. *Rainier and your mother will fall. We will all fall. What point is there in fighting?*

Live, fight, and die with honor, her father's voice answered, a distant memory translating the family crest. Her eyes lifted to the doorway, to the old Latin words etched into the stone, '*Ago pugna quod intereo per veneration*'.

They gave her strength as nothing else at the moment could. All around her, the chamber was in shambles. They'd ransacked her father's old study, knocking aside the candelabras and overturning the furniture she'd sat on so many hours as a child. Taking a blue candle that rested by her hand, she flung it at the man who spoke, knocking his foot with the hunk of wax. He merely laughed at the weak defense, kicking the candle aside.

Shiny white boots stepped closer, now smudged with the faintest trace of blue. The man leaned down, the low bass of his voice just above a whisper. "Just like your father and your brothers. Fighters all until the very end. Is it fear or pride that drives you on?"

The end?

At that she managed to lift her head, though her eyes were still on the white boots. "Rain?"

"Even the boy," the general in white answered. Josselyn caught her battered reflection in the boot, a stretched version of her face. His tone soft as a lover's, he added so only Josselyn could hear, "He died well. Have no fear of that."

Then it was true. The last of her family had fallen, save for the mother who would come home to a dried crimson river that was once her life. Would they wait for her mother? Would they kill her, too? Even as she thought it, she knew the answer. It was etched into the irritated lines of the general's face. A tear slipped over Josselyn's cheek. It would seem she still had energy enough to cry, even if she couldn't push all the way up from the floor on her own.

Josselyn gave a cold laugh. What else could she do? Tell him she hated him? Tell him he was a monster? Call him names and curse his children's children? She'd already done as much when he and his men were beating her senseless. They wanted names and she could die knowing she never gave them.

Ago pugna quod intereo per veneration.

"Get it over with," she croaked. No part of her wanted to die a failure, but her family was gone and she knew they had failed to win an impossible war. All that was left was to die well.

Was it wrong to be tired of the fight? To want

death so she may again be with those who loved her? How could she live with the loss of so much? Forget that they'd failed. Forget that soldiers were taking over the land and there was no one left to stand up to them. How could she live knowing everything she loved was gone? Pain rippled through her at the thought.

"Lift her," the general ordered, his shiny boots walking away from her, taking her reflection with it.

Two men hauled her to her feet, holding her up by her arms. Josselyn suppressed a cry as they jerked her dislocated shoulder. She couldn't see their faces, didn't need to. Her body hurt so badly she couldn't tell where the pain was coming from anymore.

The one who'd betrayed them stood before her. General Jack Stephans. He'd deceived her family and the fifth moon settlement. He'd traded them in for money and power. Josselyn lifted her gaze briefly to the hard depths of the steel green eyes before her. She wanted to kick, to give one last good blow, to go down fighting, but she couldn't raise her limbs.

"Poor little Josselyn, so heartbreaking," the general grabbed her chin and swiped beneath her eye. He looked young, was in fact very young for his position, only a few years older than her six and twenty. And yet they all knew so much more of fighting than anyone their age should, than anyone ever should.

"We gave you a home," she whispered. "How could you do this? How could you join them?"

"You gave me a place in your stables," he spat, his grip tightening on her chin, bruisingly so. "Not a place at your table. Not a place by your side. Not equal. They gave me a rank, a title. They give me respect. They give me a place in this world."

"Jack," she said, her voice softening for the orphan boy they'd found over twenty years ago. If she begged him, maybe fate could be turned around; maybe this day could be erased. Fate had spit them out in a whirlwind of chance and deceit. Maybe all that had happened wasn't his fault. Maybe it wasn't hers. None of it mattered. None of it changed the fact that he had taken everything she held dear, everyone, and now he was robbing her of her family home. Her tone hardened and she closed her eyes. "General."

"Look at me, Josselyn," he said. His tone caught even as his grip on her face tightened until his fingers pressed the inside of her cheeks against her teeth. "You're so cold. Even now, your face is composed. Is one, lonely tear all the passion you can muster?"

"I am *Lady* Josselyn of the House of Craven." Her eyes opened slowly, focusing on the shiny white of his uniform. It gleamed with the orange glow coming from the fireplace. The material looked odd in the drabber earth tones many on the fifth moon wore. Theirs was a world based on Medieval Earth. Each moon in the Florencian system was different, each settlement patterned off a singular time in the human past, times that history had almost forgotten. But the principals of the ancestors who'd established the colonies no longer applied. Times were different now. What had started as preservation of history had turned into reality, into laws and a way of life they all believed in as generation after generation was raised into the worlds of the Florencian moons.

The general shook her by the face until finally she forced her eyes to meet his. He looked angry, hurt, wildly hopeful. "I can save you. I can say you had nothing to do with the treachery of your family. No one wants to kill a woman of noble blood. The line of Craven doesn't have to die. I will take your name; the name denied me by your father."

Was he serious? She knew he'd asked her father for her hand in marriage. In fact, she'd dismissed the proposal with the full knowledge he only asked because he wanted power. Did he think she could love him now? Want him? Take him into her bed?

He must have read the answer on her face because his own expression hardened. She knew Jack. He wouldn't ask again.

"I suppose not," he said, almost sad. "Even if you agreed, I could never trust you not to take a blade to my back. Not after today." He sighed heavily. "Not after this."

"*Ago*," she whispered, even her voice beginning to fail in its strength, "*pugna quod int—*"

"Quiet your tongue! This house is mine. Mine." He let go of her chin and her head drooped. "And you can die knowing that I have taken more than what you all refused to give me in life."

"A place at our table," Josselyn said, her tone softer still, the will to live leaving her. Her heart called out to her ancestors, to her dead family, begging them to come and get her.

"My table," he corrected, stepping away. The general lifted a gun, pointing it at her head. She heard the telltale click of metal on metal. The weapon was not one found on the fifth moon. They fought with swords and axes, like the old medieval ways. Though technology was available, not using it was a point of honor. He must have brought the weapon from another moon. Perhaps the Victorians? The Elizabethans? It appeared to be too old to be from much later in time.

"Do it, Jack." She didn't look at him as she waited for the final discharge of the gun, the loud bang before the end. When it didn't come, she repeated, the words a mere mouthing of her lips, "Do it."

"Speed you to a quick end, Josselyn Craven,"

Jack whispered. "You all brought this on yourselves."

CHAPTER 2

THE CONQUEROR, DEEP SPACE, 103 YEARS LATER

"Ah-choo!"

Evan Cormier glanced up from his hand-held electronic book toward the metal ceiling of the ship commons' area. The lounge was equipped with a viewing screen, gaming tables, couches and chairs. The crew normally spent a lot of time in there, when they didn't want to be alone in their quarters. Deep space travel could be boring and they often resorted to extreme measures to alleviate the restlessness. It was rare that Evan found himself without company, but he didn't mind the others being around. Coming to the commons got him out of his room and afforded him time to read in his favorite chair.

"Princess," he acknowledged, nodding once at the metal ceiling, even though he couldn't see the petite Lintianese woman hidden behind it. A loud scrape sounded over him and within seconds the royal lady jumped down from behind a displaced grate. She landed gracefully on the floor, crouched near the ground as she looked around the room. Seeing that Evan had been alone until her arrival, the woman's dark eyes finally met his. He gave an amused half-smile and set his book aside as he studied the intruder. "What are you up to, Mei?"

Seeing Princess Mei come down from the above ducts was nothing new. She had discovered the wire-filled crawlspace when she first came aboard the spacecraft. It ran along the entire length of their ship. Back then, she'd been trying to escape Captain Jarek. Evan gave a small laugh at the thought. Jarek did eventually catch her and later married her.

If truth were known, she still jumped into the ducts to escape her husband and his all male crew. Since the rest of them couldn't fit there, the ducts had become her private sanctuary. He couldn't blame the princess. Being aboard a ship, floating in deep space with nothing but men, had to get tiring for a lady. Though, she diplomatically claimed she was fascinated with mapping out the dusty, over-head electronics graveyard of *The Conqueror*.

"Moving like the wind," Mei answered, giving a slight smile. Evan wasn't exactly sure how much of what she said was the literal truth, for Mei did have an almost supernatural connection to the breeze. She claimed it whispered secrets to her.

Mei sneezed and rubbed the tip of her nose. Dust streaked a cheek and she hardly looked like the genteel royal they'd first encountered. Before, she'd been in silken robes and had her long, dark hair plaited and pulled immaculately up on both sides of her head. Now her hair was pulled back to fall in a trail from the nape of her neck, hanging long down the line of her spine. She wore black, tight pants and a dark crimson shirt. Both hugged her like a second skin. Whenever they went onto a planet, she wore the low slinging gun belt Jarek had given her.

Mei sneezed again, her eyes watery.

"You should go spend some time in the medical unit." Evan glanced back down to his book. "All that dust can't be good for your lungs. Who knows what they used to store up there before the captain bought the ship?"

Mei frowned, and he sensed a wave of irritation. It was a strong emotion, too strong to have come just from his suggestion. She was mad at her husband. Jarek did tend to be overprotective of her, but Evan knew it was only because he loved her so much. Besides, being of Var descent, Captain Jarek was taught that women were the more fragile of the sexes and had to be taken care of. The delicate little Mei hardly needed caring for.

She'd been raised in the Imperial palace on her planet, born into not only the power of her family's rule, but into actual power. She was like the wind, free-spirited and hearing its confidences. Acting on instinct, she could handle herself and had been training in the Virtual Reality rooms to prove it.

Evan grimaced as he realized he was picking up on Mei's emotions again. For the most part, he tried not to use his 'gift' to read into the other crewmembers' personal feelings, but sometimes it was unavoidable.

"Your husband is exasperating you again, isn't he?" Evan asked, resigning himself to the interruption.

Mei nodded.

"Still fighting over what you named the baby?" he continued.

Again, she nodded.

"I know that's not what's really bothering you." Evan gave her a meaningful look. He picked up on several things from her lately, but most predominate was the need for privacy and space on certain issues.

Mei shook her head. "No, it's not."

"He loves you. He will listen."

"I know, but I must first discover what it is I wish to say. There is no air here. I cannot listen to my own thoughts blowing through me."

"He's coming this way." Evan glanced meaning-fully toward the door.

"Help me?" Mei asked, her tone soft and still burred with the accent of her birth. There was just something about the tiny woman that begged to be taken care of, and each and every member of the crew felt it. She was like their little sister.

Evan sighed and stood. Threading his hands together, he held them like a step. Mei placed her foot in his palms and lifted up, jumping to catch the end of the grate. She moved with incredible agility, especially for a woman who'd just had a baby six months ago.

Poking her head over the side, she whispered, "You didn't see me."

"Mei!" Jarek yelled, sliding to a stop at the door-way. Long, waist-length dark hair flew about his shoulders from where it was bound at the nape of his tattooed neck. It was clear he'd been running around the ship, chasing his wife. His eyes glowed, threatening with the tiger he could shift into at will. "Sacred Cats, woman, get down here and talk to me!"

"There is nothing to talk about, *ten nai*," Mei yelled just as loudly. "We are not calling our son Parker anymore."

"But that's his name," Jarek protested, his tone giving away how exasperated he was. "Besides, you liked it when we were at your parents' house. Your father even announced it as the baby's name before he was born. What else are we to call him?"

"Well, it annoys me now. If you keep saying it to him, he'll think it is his name for real." Mei's voice was muffled, and they could hear her crawling away from them.

"Well," Jarek paused, sending a wave of frustration over Evan. "It is his name for real. Read the birth announcements."

"You put those out before I could agree to it, before he was even born." Her voice had gotten faint and Evan knew she was already quite a long ways down the duct.

"Irritating *fea*," Jarek mumbled. "I cannot help it if I was excited. He was halfway born when I sent the transmission to my family."

Evan laughed, taking his seat once more. "I thought you'd decided on Parker before the birth."

"We did," Jarek grumbled. "Emperor Zhang is pressuring her for a family name to be added to Parker. I told her we could name him after my twin brother, Reid. Sacred Cats, any of my brothers for that matter, but she wants a Lintianese royal name. I'm sorry, but I'm not calling my son Jin. I knew a Je'en once and she was three hundred pounds of slime. I'm not calling my son that. His Var cousins will beat him up for it."

"It's only a second name," Evan reasoned, knowing that Jarek's nieces and nephews would do no such thing—at least not in earnest. Var family ties were too strong. Evan often felt jealousy when Jarek was near his family, not jealousy on the captain's part, but his own. Aside from his friends, Evan had no true family. It wasn't so much that his friends weren't good enough, as they were family in a way, but only being around Jarek and his brothers made him miss the family he'd lost.

"I know. I'll probably give in, but the woman keeps running away from me whenever I try to discuss it." Jarek sighed. "I want to know what this is really about first before I start agreeing to changing my son's name or adding to it, or whatever other crazy idea she has in mind. I know Parker's name really isn't what's troubling her, but she won't talk to me."

Evan didn't answer. He knew better than to get into the middle of people's affairs, especially when the heart was involved. Jarek looked at him, hopeful. His voice flat, he said, "I'm not reading your wife, so don't ask."

Jarek gave him a funny look and said dryly, "Enough about me. What you reading now?"

Evan passed his hand-held reader over to Jarek so the captain could see the screen.

"*The Practical Impact of Lintianese Elements on*

Everyday Life—a translation from the original text," Jarek read, shaking his head. "You're still dwelling on that prediction, aren't you?"

"Just trying to make sense out of what Zhang An said." Evan sighed, taking the hand-held from Jarek.

Zhang An was the ancestral spirit of Mei's Imperial family. Rick Hayes, their pilot, had angered the spirit and, as a punishment for his insults, she had partially predicted some of the crews' futures. The punishment part wasn't the reading, but the cryptic way in which it was done. Truth was, Evan didn't think there was any way to translate the ominous divination. He'd come to the conclusion that An had only said what she did to mess with them. It was working. He could think of little else since.

Closing his eyes, Evan leaned back in his cushioned seat as he remembered the day An had predicted their futures. The ability to remember things with crystal clarity was one of his gifts—or so he was told. There were some memories he wished would fade with time, some things he'd rather not see again, and it was hard to consider those vivid memories a gift.

A wave passed over the darkness under his lids and a blurry vision of what had once been came to him. The image of the past cleared, and he could see things just as he'd seen them when they happened.

Jarek had just brought Mei home to her parents. The two had been in love, but didn't think they could be together. Mei was a Lintianese princess and Jarek was a Var prince who, for all intents and purposes, didn't use his title. Instead, he went by captain and kept to the high skies as a borderline pirate balancing on the edge between law and outlaw. Jarek was still loyal to his family, but the prince knew he had to live his own life. It took Mei awhile to learn the same, but here she was with all of them, wandering the universes in search of whatever it was they all sought.

Evan took a deep breath, listening to the past for clues and knowing it would bring none.

'*Whoa, easy there, ghostly sweetness,*' a remembered voice whispered in his head. It had been Rick speaking, insulting the ancestral spirit. He was the ship's pilot and a talented one at that. For all his devil-may-care attitude and rakish demeanor, Rick really was a good man. He'd give his life for anyone of his friends, just as they would give their life for him. But caring for the man like a brother didn't change the fact that he was downright infuriating at times. Evan knew Rick only said what he did to the old spirit to draw attention away from the captain at a tense moment, but the spirit hadn't taken kindly to the insolent tone.

Evan kept his eyes closed, trying to remember each detail of what had happened. It wasn't hard. He thought about it every day.

'I will teach you respect, little man. You will bow in the presence of my greatness... Do not make me curse you.' An's spectral figure had glistened with light as her anger grew. Long, dark hair streaked with white flowed around her shoulders. Her sleeves swept over the ground as she drifted slightly over them. The delicate silk of her gown was made even more so by the fact that it traveled on air. Every movement was silent, like the breeze.

Evan had tried to get Rick to be quiet, but it didn't work. The man always pushed things a little too far, going on to perversely comment about the woman's gown getting twisted or some such nonsense. Since Rick had a thing for twenty-first century Earth memorabilia and sayings, they couldn't always figure out what some of his expressions meant. The old spirit might have just let him go with a small personal curse, but Rick then made some comment about her powers or lack thereof. Instead of just bringing her curse upon himself, Rick caused her wrath to turn to the other members of Jarek's crew—at least those unfortunate enough to be present at the time. Evan, Lochlann, Jackson, and Dev still didn't fully forgive Rick for what had happened next.

An's eyes had turned white, as she foretold just a tiny piece of their future, '*Together you travel and together you'll remain. Tied and joined like the five elements of our people. The road to happiness is very rocky for all of you.*' When her eyes had cleared, indicating she'd come out of her vision, she'd smiled vindictively at them. '*You will find your love hidden within the mystery of the five elements. One element for each of you. The corresponding element will hold the secret to your future happiness. But fate is not clear. If you do not recognize it, you will lose it and be forever alone.*'

Since Evan was unable to psychically read spirits, he didn't know if she was lying or not. Part of him hoped she was, but in truth it didn't matter. Her words served their purpose. They tormented with just a glimpse of the unknown and no real guidance as to what it could mean. That was the true curse, not knowing the rest or what could be done about it.

Zhang An obviously had great powers. She could have told them more, could have said which element was assigned to each man, could have said when, where, more of the how. No, all they got was the ominous, '*If you do not recognize it, you will lose it and be forever alone.*' Now, the secret to their future happiness rested in the mystery of the five Lintianese elements.

"Mei says it will come to you as soon as you stop dwelling on it," Jarek offered, drawing Evan from his thoughts, back into the present. "She also said that the words are not literal, but figurative. It could be a nuance of the intended's personality or she could love water or fire. Sacred Cats, the wood element could merely mean the woman was born at the same time a tree was felled outside her birth room door. It is impossible to tell. You should take your mind from it and live as you have. Nothing has changed."

Nothing? Evan wanted to laugh and scream at the same time.

"How? There is nothing to do on this ship and seeing you happily married doesn't help matters." Evan shut off the reader and set it aside. He had read book after book and they all said the same thing. Five Elements—fire, earth, wood, water, and metal. Simple and complex. Infinite possibilities. Ultimate insanity.

But how could Evan stop looking? Zhang An's words threatened the very thing he wanted most— to once again have a family. He wanted a family of his own so badly that the idea of missing his chance, of walking by the woman he should be looking for, tore at him.

Jarek laughed dryly as he looked to where his wife had disappeared. "Yeah, right. Happy."

"Love her. That is all you can do." Evan relented a little as he said just enough to ease Jarek's overbearing worry for his wife. "I think we all need a diversion, even Mei."

"Such as?"

"We need to find some mischief to occupy our time." Evan gave a sly grin. "Want to go kidnap your brother again? That was entertaining."

"Again?" Jarek shook his head. "No, you are not laying that deed upon my head. That was under Samantha's command. She was your captain on that fated mission."

"At least it was fated to end well." Evan chuckled. "Samantha and Falke did marry."

"This will end well, too." Jarek motioned toward the book Evan had turned off. "You're too good for the gods not to bless you."

Evan wished he had such blind certainty. The Var never seemed to struggle when it came to faith in a higher power. To them it just was, as real as the green-tinted sky stretching over their planet of Qurilixen.

Evan watched the captain leave, knowing Jarek was going to try and track his wayward wife down.

'If you do not recognize it, you will lose it and be forever alone.'

That statement haunted his dreams. Five elements for the five single crewmen who had stood before her. Unluckily, Evan was one of the five. If Rick hadn't saved his life so many times in the past, he would've thrown him off the spaceship thousands of miles away from any planet. The others were in the exact same situation as he was. Rick had saved them all more times than they could count, and that wasn't including the numerous times he'd flown them out of a dangerous chase. Well, admittedly, the number was significantly lower for the crewmen Lochlann and Jackson. The two men were originally part of Captain Jarek's crew.

Evan, Rick, Dev and the two brothers, Lucien and Viktor, were all originally part of Captain Samantha Dorsey's crew. When Sam married the kidnapped Prince Falke and chose to stay with him on his home planet, they were left without a ship or a captain. Prince Jarek, Falke's brother, needed a crew and they needed a captain. It worked out perfectly for all.

Evan's stomach tightened, as his thoughts turned to Sam in perfect detail. She had saved his life long ago. It was an old, painful wound and a memory he didn't like to visit. In that memory, he'd lost everything—his family, wealth, legacy. Sam had been his bright spot, his reason for living. She'd nearly died to save him, and in turn, he'd nursed her back to health. Out of all the things he had, she was the most important. Though she was happily married and well taken care of, living like a princess, Evan missed her. Even so, he wouldn't change her fate. Never would he take a friend's happiness for his own.

"Holy Space Balls!" Rick's voice intruded on Evan's thoughts, startling him. The pilot grimaced, halfway into the commons as his brown eyes widen in mock concern. "You're dwelling, aren't you? Now, don't lie. I can see it in your furrowed brow. You're not going to try and beat me up again, are you?"

Evan frowned. "I didn't try to beat you up."

"Yeah, but you didn't stop Jackson and Lochlann from having a go at me, did you?" Rick grinned, his expression saying he was hardly concerned.

"You talking about me?" Lochlann asked, suddenly appearing at the door. He was a dragon shifter, a Draig, who came from the same planet as Captain Jarek. The two were longtime friends who had run away from home while their two races were at war. Neither one of them had wanted to fight so they chose the high skies. In space, things like a person's race didn't matter as much. Everyone was different. Though the war on Qurilixen was over, Lochlann and Jarek's families didn't fully accept their friendship.

"No," Rick lied.

"Hmm, 'cause I'll beat your ass again." Lochlann laughed. "Just for the fun of it."

"I'll help him." Jackson joined them, falling onto a seat with a big sigh. He was a security officer who kept mostly to himself. Evan knew he was a good man, could feel it with his 'gifts'. Jackson spent a lot of his time in the Virtual Reality training room with Dev, fighting computer-simulated beasts. Evan knew Jackson had plenty of his own demons to fight.

"Ah." Rick waved his hand in dismissal. "Shut your black holes."

"What's all the yelling about?" Viktor asked, carrying a tray of Qurilixen blue bread and a steaming bowl of liquid for dipping. Lucien and Viktor had gotten lucky. When the rest of the crew was cursed, they'd stayed on the ship guarding a prisoner while the others were at the Zhang palace.

"Lucky bastards," Evan mumbled to himself at the thought.

"Who's the bastard?" Lucien joined them, moving by to swipe the tray from his brother for himself. Viktor protested, as Lochlann and Rick moved to block his pursuit. Lucien tossed pieces of bread to his helpers, only to hand Viktor back the empty tray.

The two brothers constantly bickered even though they were really quite close. They were half human, half dere, and had a milky white complexion which contrasted the strangest red-brown and red-green of their eyes. Lucien was a communications genius and Viktor was one hell of a mechanic.

"You are," Viktor grumbled, eyeing his empty tray. Turning toward the door, he added, "Good thing I fixed the food simulator."

"Hey, bring me something," Jackson yelled. Viktor waved his hand over his head by way of an answer. The three bread-thieving men chewed on their stolen goods as Jackson and Evan watched.

"So? What's the yelling about?" Lucien asked, popping the last bit of bread into his mouth.

"Jarek and Mei." Evan didn't need to expand upon the comment.

"What's with you?" Lucien asked.

"He's dwelling on what that old bag of air said," Rick answered. Then to Evan, he added, "Why worry about it? I bet she couldn't predict her way out of the palace, let alone tell us what our future holds. Holy space balls, she couldn't even walk toward the light when she died and now is stuck annoying people. She's just a dead broad, that doesn't mean she's smart."

Evan quirked a brow. "Then why were you trying to make amends with the rest of us last time we were on Lintian?"

Rick shrugged. "She's pretty sexy for an older lady and I've never done it with a ghost."

He looked so sincere, and they couldn't help but laugh at him.

"I'm sure it's just like having sex with air," Jackson said thoughtfully. "And you've done that often enough."

Rick lifted his hand, wiggling his fingers. "Never air, space cadet. I've got my favorite lady right here."

"Maybe old Zhang An is your fate," Lucien teased. The two dere brothers had enjoyed tormenting 'the cursed ones' to no end. "You've got the element of air."

Rick shivered. "Married to an old dove like that? Spare me the horror."

"Dove?" Jackson asked. "Broad? Walking toward light?"

"It's a—" Rick began.

"Never mind, I don't want to know," Jackson said. "I think it's better if we don't get your meanings."

"I'm not fated to be air," Rick informed Lucien. "It's pretty obvious that I'm metal." He pounded his chest. "Hard as ship's steel."

"Your head is full of air," Evan mumbled. If the old spirit had wanted to drive them to madness, she'd picked a brilliant way of doing it. Being part telepath, Evan knew the dangers of revealing too much of the future, but there was also danger in not saying enough. It's why he often said nothing about what he sensed in others, or what fate had in store. In fact, the other crewmembers didn't exactly know how much of the future he could see. But, since tomorrow was forever changing, it was pointless for him to give hints and change fate. Intentions could be misread. Knowing the future often changed the way people acted and could sometimes cause dangerous outcomes.

"Ah, stop being so melancholy. You should be happy to know how to avoid marriage," Rick said. "Can you imagine? Being bound to one woman? I like Mei, but I feel sorry for Jarek. Forced to sleep in one woman's bed for the rest of his life, stuck banging the same piece of—"

"Rick," Evan warned.

"Hand?" Lucien finished for Rick, chuckling.

Rick gave them an ornery look and kissed his knuckles. Whispering to his hand, he said, "Don't listen to him, sweetness, he didn't mean it."

"The captain's in love. Why feel sorry for him?" Jackson asked, though the look on his face wasn't as certain as his tone.

"Jackson, come. I've reset the program." Dev appeared at the entryway and Jackson instantly stood.

"Ah, lay off, would you, Dev," Rick grumbled. "I'm trying to start a party here."

"I don't want any part of the party you're trying to start," Viktor teased.

"The last time you started something, we kidnaped a prince," Dev answered. He was the ship's muscle and a bit of a loner. Being of half Belvon descent, Dev was of a demonic looking race with red skin and a very stern temperament. Aside from the intense coloring, he appeared humanoid, only larger. Because of his human features, the Belvon rejected him and, because of his Belvon features, the humans feared him. He was an outcast to either race, but on this ship, he was a brother. Rick was the opposite of Dev. The Belvon was all about maintaining order and Rick was all about breaking it.

"And Sam got married to him," Lucien said. "It worked out."

Evan felt his gut tighten again at the mention of her name.

"That gives me an idea." Rick winked at the group in general, as he crossed toward the gaming table. "Wanna play Kiss My Comet? We could always see what we kidnap next? You never know, we might find a sexy woman with five breasts locked in one of our quarters tomorrow morning."

"We're not drunk," Evan said, by way of

denying the request to play a kid's game. It's the only thing the crew could remember the rules to when they were blitzed.

"Mm, not yet," Rick corrected, reaching behind a seat and pulling out a half-full bottle of Earth whiskey. "But that's easily rectified."

"It's early," Lochlann protested, even as he stood.

"Not on the west side of Qurilixen." Rick grinned. "Come on, it'll take your mind off of that stupid premonition."

"Jackson?" Dev asked.

"Yeah, coming." Jackson followed Dev out of the commons.

"You need space credits again, don't you?" Evan laughed.

"I do," Rick admitted. Then, lowering his voice, he said, "I just picked up a loose transmission wave in the cockpit. Rumor has it the Galaxy Playmates are doing a show near the Siren Mining Colony. If we have just the right amount of engine trouble, his royal princeliness will have to let us land there for repairs."

"You're going to sabotage our ship?" Evan quirked a brow.

"Ah, sabotage is such a harsh word." Rick took a long pull off the whiskey bottle. "I'd like to think of it as saving the crew. Ever since Jarek got married, or mated, or whatever it is those Var do, he hasn't put in for any shore leave." He paused, motioning down to his crotch. "Little Rick is feeling mighty neglected these days. He's not too happy."

"Watch a download," Evan quipped, reaching for the bottle. He paused, looking at the old fashioned label on it to make sure it wasn't anything strange.

"Not as fun as the real thing." Rick grabbed the bottle back to take another swig, his look telling all that the whiskey was untainted. He started to drink, but Lucien swiped it from him, spilling liquor down Rick's chin. "I keep saving up to buy one of those pleasure android girls I saw Lochlann looking at, but I can never seem to hold onto enough money. In fact, I think I might end up lifting one next time I get the chance."

"We are not kidnapping anyone or anything tonight." Lucien took a drink. "I don't want that kind of adventure. Besides, pleasure robots, droids, whatever you want to call them, are chipped. I heard if you steal one and then try to use it without the right codes, it'll blow your manhood right off. It's a built in security measure." Then to Evan, he added under his breath, "Unless this time the adventure leads to Rick getting married and left behind."

"Ha, ha." Rick pretended to growl as he took

the bottle of whiskey away and passed it again to Evan. "I miss Sam. She would've played cards with me. And she would've gone to Siren just for the adventure of it. She had the best ideas, like the time she entered us in the great space race."

All but Lochlann laughed. He'd not been part of their crew when it happened.

"And, as far as the future Mrs. Rick Hayes is concerned," Rick continued. "Viktor can overwrite any programming glitch she might have."

"You'd put your balls in my brother's hands?" Lucien snickered, knowing just how bad the question sounded.

Rick growled at him. "Keep it up, space cadet. I know the launch codes to the pods. I'll shoot you so far into deep space you'll—"

"Finally get some peace because I won't have to listen to you run your mouth all day?" Lucien offered.

Evan took a drink and then another before handing the bottle back. "Sam and Falke. Funny how things work out, eh?"

"Yeah. Funny." Rick's face turned serious for a brief moment before again lifting into an easy smile.

"I'll deal." Lucien pulled a chair to the gaming table.

"You cheat," Lochlann said, doing the same. "I'll deal."

"Do not," Lucien protested.

"Yeah, you do," Viktor said from the door. This time he carried a huge tray, overflowing with food. He set it down in front of them.

"Sam wasn't the woman for you," Rick said, leaning close so only Evan could hear. Though he didn't look it, Evan could feel the concern in his friend. Rick placed his hand on the arm of Evan's chair, leaning over him. "She never was."

Evan nodded.

"She is Falke's wife, Jarek's sister-by-marriage," Rick reiterated, handing up the bottle. "And our *friend*."

Evan nodded again. He knew all that and didn't need the reminder. "Enough, I'm fine about it." Then louder, he said, "Now, let me deal the hand. I'm the only one of us who doesn't cheat and I don't want to stop playing until we all pass out."

"That's the spirit," Rick clapped his hands. "And I promise you won't regret it!"

CHAPTER 3

EVAN DIDN'T MOVE as he stared up at the commons' metal ceiling. Getting drunk had been a rash, horrible decision and he regretted making it. His head throbbed, radiating pain through his temples, his eyes, his neck and shoulders. Beyond that, he couldn't feel anything.

"All right, you've suffered enough." Mei's voice came from a fog, booming abnormally loud for the soft-spoken woman.

Evan felt a tug on his arm and several burning pokes. By small degrees, he started to feel better. The ache lessened and his eyes no longer hurt when he blinked. Turning his clearing head toward the princess, he saw her holding the hand-held medic unit to his arm and weakly nodded his thanks.

"I should leave the lot of you to rot in misery, but I found something," Mei said.

Evan mumbled, but even he didn't know what he was trying to say.

"In the ducts," Mei explained. "It's old. Really old. Well, old like my husband at any rate."

"I'm in the prime of my life," Jarek's voice protested.

"Mm, yes you are," Mei agreed.

"I've got hundreds of years left in me," Jarek continued.

"Whatever you say, *ten nai*." Mei giggled, teasing him.

Evan pulled himself up, the slow movements of his body hampered by the lingering grogginess in his head. He'd slept on the floor and had the stiff muscles to prove it. Blinking several times, Mei's words registered. "What did you find? Another broken communicator? Or a phaser?"

"No," Jarek said. "She really did find something this time."

Evan glanced at the captain. He'd spent the evening with his wife and it looked like they'd worked out whatever they'd been fighting over.

"*Fea*, get the others so we can all look at its contents," Jarek told his wife. "Please."

She nodded, moving toward Lucien and Viktor

with the hand-held medical unit. Soon the others were moaning as they came to.

Evan rubbed the back of his neck. "What did she find?"

"*She* found an old holographic box," Mei answered.

"It looks political, maybe fifty or so years old," Jarek added.

"What's a political holo-box doing on this ship?" Evan frowned. "There wasn't any mention when you bought it that it was once a Federation ship, was there?"

"There wasn't mention of anything when I came in possession of this ship," Jarek admitted. "The guy who had it before me didn't have the original ship's logs so we just kind of..."

"Made them up," Jackson offered bluntly.

"Made them up?" Mei repeated.

Jarek shrugged, unapologetic. "The ship was a bargain."

"A holo-box?" Lucien and Viktor said in unison.

"It could be weapon schematics," Lucien said. "Or some stolen piece of evidence."

"I'll know if it's a weapon," Viktor countered. "There is only so much the Federation could do with weaponry that long ago."

"Fine, but if you blow us up with that old—" Lucien couldn't finish.

"Hey, fifty years is not that long ago," Jarek protested.

"Whatever you say, pops," Rick laughed.

"Pops?" Jarek repeated. "I don't know what you're calling me, but I'm sure I'll put a fist in your face if I ever find out."

"Ah, stop arguing," Rick grouched. "My head still hurts."

"No one made you down that entire bottle by yourself," Lochlann said.

"We need Dev," Mei made a move for the door. "He's with Par—*my son*. I'll go get him."

"What's with her lately?" Jackson asked. Jarek waved his hand and they all knew better than to pry.

Jackson's green eyes were rimmed with red and he looked like someone had punched him in the jaw. Evan vaguely remembered a punching game of cards the night before. He glanced at Rick. The man had a matching bruise near his left eye. Yep, they'd had a game where the person with the losing hand got punched. Good thing he was too smart for that foolishness.

"You guys look like you've been to battle," Jarek smirked, motioning to Rick's face. "Now, Rick I understand. We all want to hit him."

"Hey," Rick protested, gingerly touching his eye.

"I can't help it you're jealous of my dazzling good looks."

"And Jackson is always bruised from the VR training." Jarek pointed at Jackson before giving a pointed look at Evan. "But you, Evan? I expected more out of you."

Evan frowned, stood up, and went toward the metal wall where Rick had buffed it to a polished sheen. Seeing his reflection, he grimaced. A sharp pain radiated down the side of his face, and he instantly relaxed the muscles. Both of his eyes were bruised and the bridge of his nose appeared swollen. No wonder he felt like he'd been dragged behind a space ship. He turned back around to look at the other crewmen.

"What?" Rick said to him, smiling innocently. "You had a lousy run of luck."

"Come on, let's go get some food into you men," Jarek said. "You'll think better with clearer heads and fuller stomachs. I'll have Mei meet us in there with the holo-box."

As Jarek left, Evan made a move to follow behind. Rick came up beside him and slung an arm around his shoulders. "So, my little friend. I hope you weren't too drunk last night and forgot our bet."

"Bet?" Evan repeated, not liking the sound of that.

"Yes, bet. You promised to read the next sexy

woman we saw and tell me all her deepest sexual fantasies." Rick grinned.

Evan pushed the man's arm off of him. "I would never bet any such thing."

As he walked toward the dining hall, curious to see Mei's newest treasure, he heard Rick laugh, "Well, can't blame me for trying."

"Top secret. Prisoner two, two, five release order number six, nine, twelve. This is General Stephans of the New Earth Settlement on Florencia's Fifth Moon." The small image of the holographic general paused as he stood in shiny white on the round disc on top of the old metal holo-box. The miniature man's fingers ran through his dark hair before his hand again fell to the side. "This is General Stephans of what was *formerly* the Earth Settlement on Florencia's Fifth Moon and this is an official order of..." The holographic image blipped and faded. General Stephans's image froze in mid-motion, his mouth agape.

"I didn't know Florencia had more than one moon, let alone settlements on it," Lucien said. "It's just a dead planet, isn't it?"

They all gathered in the dining hall. Plates of half

eaten food were strewn over the table as they all sat around the holo-box. It had taken most of the meal for Viktor to bypass the codes and get it running and even longer until the message would play with sound. Dev stood behind Mei, his arms crossed over his chest. Mei lounged against her husband's side, even as the couple managed to stay seated in their own chairs. Jackson and Lochlann leaned against the counter, drinking some kind of thick pink substance that Evan didn't even want to know the ingredients of. They claimed it was an old remedy to help the head, but he wasn't that desperate to get rid of the ache between his eyes.

"If the old geography upload I had when I was a child still serves, there were several moons to the planet, like ten or twelve." Evan looked up. "Florencia's Fifth Moon? I thought that was an ice prison. I thought they were all ice prisons."

"It didn't used to be," Jackson answered. "A long time ago they were each inhabited by human settlements. I knew a guy who was born on the fourth planet. He was an old timer and probably dead by now, but he said they were established by humans and set up like periods of Old Earth history. People were afraid that they'd forget the ways of Old Earth when they abandoned the dying planet for New Earth."

"Like a tourist moon system?" Lucien mused.

"Exactly." Jackson nodded. "Now it's an ice prison."

"I've heard of this place. They froze prisoners in blocks of ice or something." Viktor stiffened even as he rubbed his head in thought. "Weren't the prisons abandoned? I remember hearing something, somewhere about how the prisoners were being slowly defrosted without the aid of medical personnel and then they were killed by some crazy warden if they survived the painful unfreezing process."

Evan leaned forward, studying the frozen man. His transparent image made it hard to see the details of his face.

"Oh, yeah," Lucien interjected. "I remember hearing about that. He was also killing them while still frozen, smashing them, dropping them onto rocks."

"Those were just rumors," Jackson said. "You know, folk tales to scare children and keep people from attempting prison breaks."

"I don't know. I seem to remember the source being credible," Viktor said.

"You didn't happen to meet this source while drinking on some random fueling dock, did you?" Dev mused.

"Actually," Lucien interjected smartly. "It was a space port. And we weren't drunk."

"The guy was," Viktor corrected, as he fiddled

with side controls to the box. The others snickered. Reaching to the disc, he tapped the base at the man's feet several times. It flickered, but finally the holographic man continued speaking.

"...release authorized by my superiors and hereby given to the commanding warden in Ice Complex Five, Authorization code H forty-seven, fifty-one. When the ice storms came nearly forty years ago, many of my men were killed. It was too cold to stay and finish our work releasing certain political prisoners and we abandoned post on supreme orders. However, there are a few who remain that should not, as they have been pardoned for their crimes. Attached is a list of prisoners set for immediate release. They will be hostile and should be escorted and left on the Rifflen base in the V Quadrant. No provisions beyond those orders are necessary."

Evan watched every movement of the general, his eyes carefully studying the flickering man. It was frustrating, not being able to read the holographic image. Glancing around, he saw the rest of the crew was waiting for the little figure to continue talking.

When it didn't, Viktor said, "Well, it's old, right? They've probably released whatever prisoners they were supposed to." He gave a nervous laugh.

A sense of deep sadness washed over the crew. Evan knew exactly why they felt that way. The idea of some person being stuck because of a lost communication was a horrific possibility.

"What if they're still there, frozen, because this message was lost?" Jackson whispered. "Can you imagine? Fifty years in an ice block?"

"Could be longer than that," Viktor said. "Who knows how long they were in ice before they were pardoned."

"It's too late," Jackson whispered. "Their bodies probably decomposed within the ice blocks. I'd logically assume that most humanoid bodies can't be frozen for that long and survive."

"The prisoners might not be human," Lucien said. "Just because the settlement that came before was human doesn't mean the prisoners all are."

"Are we sure they froze the prisoners in ice?" Jarek asked.

Evan's concentration was broken by another emotion, a deeper one. Blinking in surprise, he noticed for the first time since the transmission had started that Rick hadn't moved. He was staring at the little, blinking figure, his face white. Pain rolled over Evan, more intense than any emotion he'd ever picked up from Rick. It was like some door had squeaked open just a crack inside of the man.

Gasping, Evan clutched his chest. "Rick? What...?"

Just as suddenly, the door inside Rick slammed shut and Evan could breathe.

"Evan? Are you all right?" Mei shot to her feet amidst the sound of her chair scraping across the floor. She was instantly by his side. "What happened? You're as pale as my dead ancestors."

"Rick?" Evan asked again. All eyes turned to the man. Rick gave an easy smile, but Evan saw something different in his expression, something he'd never noticed before.

"Let's go check it out." Rick's blackened eyes hid all expression. "It couldn't hurt to inquire; at least drop off the release orders if anyone is still there on guard. Let them handle their own matters."

"But—?" Evan couldn't speak. He was too stunned by what he'd felt in the man.

"You want to go on a rescue mission?" Lucien broke in, his tone revealing how shocked he was.

"Could be a women's prison." Rick winked.

"Evan?" Mei asked softly.

"I'm fine," he assured her and she backed away, again joining her husband's side.

"I'll go set the coordinates. If memory serves, it's only a couple days' flight from where we're at, week at most." Rick crossed over the table, not giving another glance at the holo-box. He whistled a light tune, sounding very much like his old self.

"Something's wrong," Evan said, staring after the pilot.

"Ah," Jarek waved a dismissing hand. "Something is always off with Rick. It's what makes Rick, Rick." Then, putting his fists on his hips, he said, "All right, let's get ready for anything. Dev, Jackson, you two make sure all the weapons are charged and ready. You never know what we'll find once we're down there. Fifty years is a long time. Viktor, you see if you can't figure out the rest of that thing, if there even is a rest. We'll need those prisoner numbers. Lochlann, you and Evan go through our winter supplies and take inventory. An ice prison complex? Sounds cold. Lucien, you're on research. Find out what you can about Ice Complex Five. Once Viktor gets the numbers, hopefully you'll be able to find something out about whom we are supposed to rescue. I don't want to thaw any savage killers and set them loose on the galaxies."

CHAPTER 4

ICE COMPLEX FIVE, FLORENCIA'S FIFTH MOON, ONE WEEK LATER...

EVAN PULLED his coat tighter to his chest. Their snowsuits came in two parts. The thick, black padding was surprisingly lightweight for all the bulk. Federation patches were sewn along the chests on all but Jackson's white suit, which read ESC for the Exploratory Science Commission. They'd "scavenged" the suits like just about everything else on their ship. Technically, the load of winter supplies had been abandoned when they found it, even if it had a lock on the cargo box and sat next to an unused ESC compound. Beneath their suits, they wore "borrowed" ESC skintight black jumpsuits. The undergarment molded to their bodies, covering arms and legs completely for added protection against the elements. The material was so elastic, it even stretched to fit Dev, though his snowsuit was modified and appeared a little short on him. The under suits came with a transmitter sewn into the v-neckline, which Viktor modified to connect the ground crew to their ship by way of a primitive radio signal.

The cold wintry air had a severe bite as it hit Evan's exposed cheeks and nose. Whoever had designated the moon for the ice prisons couldn't have picked a better location. Rotating the uninhabited planet of Florencia, the moon had been cultivated to sustain life, and by the appearances of the icy tundra, had also fallen into desolation, abandoning the life it once supported.

The pale blue-grey of the sky was clear and long, stretching for miles without a single thing to mar its flat color. The weather was no surprise. When they'd approached in their ship, they'd scanned the area. There were twelve moons and a planet with only one sun to warm them. Though old weather shuttles looked as if they'd once regulated the seasons, amplifying the sun, a hole had been blown in the side of the one that rotated around the Fifth Moon and now circled as a useless mass of junk. It was even too old to scavenge for parts.

On the surface, icy sculptures of the past stood in frozen testament. What looked to be rows of crops lined the gentle swooping landscape. They were unharvested, trampled along the edge by foot-prints leading to a square metal building which was the prison. The newer prison complex was severely out of place with the rest of the small moon's older style structures. There was no reason to its place-ment, as if built in a hurry with no care to the surrounding nature. What had been an orchard of trees stretched to its side, the limbs slick and shiny like icicles poking toward the heavens.

"It's like the gods sculpted it from ice and set it down," Jackson whispered.

"More like cursed it once it was built, sheathing it in ice," Jarek said.

Trekking from where their ship lifted off the ground to hover above in space, they made their way into the prison complex. Mei was still on the spaceship with her son and Lochlann to keep her company. The man had lost the random draw and was left behind as the rest of them went in search of the prisoners. Mei wasn't too happy about not going along, but Jarek had given her little choice in the matter, appealing to her motherly instinct.

The compound was unlocked, the sensors down. After a quick sweep for alarms, they pushed inside. For the most part, the building was abandoned, cold square rooms, standing forgotten and not very unlike other prison compounds he'd seen—espe-cially those built by the Federation a century ago.

Almost every surface was made of flat, metal, standard Federation issue building supplies. The compound was cold, but the snow did not penetrate the metal walls and ceiling. Lights gave them plenty to see by, the prison system still running off of an old biocell. After throwing the main switch by the front door, sensors detected them as they entered each room, automatically switching on power to all the room's systems.

Evan wasn't sure what they had expected to find, but he had carried a picture in his mind of solid blocks of ice with prisoners trapped inside, or a plastic-type holding containers, even a fluid filled tube with computers monitoring the vitals of the floating prisoners within. Instead, they found eerie statues, locked in fear, in screams, arms raised as if to protect their faces. What solid evidence they'd found of prisoners was disturbing, lending credence to the rumors that they'd been killed while still frozen in stone. Many of the unfortunate souls were broken, skulls crushed, heads knocked off, limbs crumbling into piles of red tinted stones. Not really ice, but more like cool rocks, they were the perfect prisoners. They didn't eat, didn't sleep, didn't talk or complain. They merely stood, unmoving, helpless in a large court in the center of the building.

"They look to be in pain," Viktor whispered, as he touched a disembodied head. The woman's lips were wide in a scream and her eyes were shut tight. "Do you think these were really people?"

"They were people," Dev answered grimly.

"Why's this room so dusty? The rest of the compound is spotless," Lucien said. He'd taken off his dark cap, exposing his head to the chill. A flush brightened his cheeks, matching those of his companions.

"It's the stones. No one cleaned up after they were destroyed," Dev answered.

"You mean we're stepping in..." Viktor froze, looking down to where his feet left prints in the fine dust. "People?"

"Looks like it." Jackson frowned, nudging a young man with his foot. The boy couldn't have been more than thirteen human years with long, floppy hair that covered his stone eyes. "This one has phazer blasts in the stomach and chest. If they were used as target practice, repeatedly shot at, that would account for the dust."

"They don't exactly look like criminals." Evan's stomach churned. The emotions churning inside him weren't his alone. Every one of them felt the same. There was no love between them and anything Federation, but to see these people caused a wave of disgust and sorrow. The crew might be space pirates, but they had hearts. "In fact, they look like regular people."

"What are criminals supposed to look like?" Lucien mused.

"I only mean that these people look like they come from the same place." Evan motioned toward a woman on the floor. Her dress was perfectly intact, even if half of her head and hands were missing. The long gown and apron were plain, but seemed to indicate a style similar to the men, with their loose fitted pants and long, tunic-like shirts. "They're dressed in the same style of clothing, like they came from the same planet."

"I count about twenty-five prisoners." Dev knelt at the feet of one of the more composed males. The older gentleman was locked in what appeared to be prayer, his hands clasped and his face gritted but composed—at least the lower half that was still attached to his neck. Dev swiped his hand over the dusty floor. "The lot numbers are at the base of each prisoner." He walked along what would have made an even row, running his foot through the dust. "Over half of them are missing. There are lot numbers but no sign of the prisoner to go with it."

"Unless they're dust," Jackson said.

"Or the rumors about the warden were true," Viktor offered, "and they were thawed without medical supervision."

"We'll check the medic logs. They have to have prison records somewhere and that's the most logical place to start," Jarek decided. Though he didn't say it, Evan knew they all were especially curious to discover what had come of the persons meant to be pardoned. They had only been able to retrieve one and a half numbers.

"I didn't know they kept prisons like this," Lucien said. "It makes me like the Federation even less."

"I don't think they do anymore," Rick said. "If they did, this place would still be running. It's the perfect location—far out of the way, dead, and forgotten."

"Look at how all the statues are crushed," Dev said, his tone flat and matter-of-fact. "Why execute them unless it was to hide the secret of this place?" Then, in disgust, he spat, "Cowards, killing them without doing the honor of putting a weapon in their hand."

"Unless they were deadly," Jarek said, though he didn't sound convinced. He crouched down beside a woman who had been severed in two. He touched her cheek, tracing what looked to be a frozen tear. Evan trembled, forced to look away. He felt the men's pity and frustration. It compounded his own.

"Odds are," Jackson said, "they figured whoever found it would assume these were really just broken statues and not prisoners."

"Come on, let's see if we can find the logs and

make sure there isn't any missing or hidden somewhere else. I can't imagine leaving anyone to this fate." Jarek made a move to continue through the facility.

"I don't think they feel anything," Jackson said.

"I should hope not," Evan whispered. He noticed Rick didn't say anything, merely stood, looking around.

"Let's be sure," Jarek ordered. "We came here so we might as well see this through. Keep your eyes open for removable property."

After searching the facility and finding none that could be thawed without instantly dying from their injuries, they located the medical laboratory. Viktor accessed the computer, unable to bypass many of the old military codes. In the end, they found an old hand-held with a master list of all lot numbers, but no crimes or names. Anyone who didn't know what to look for would think them cargo lot numbers. But, what they discovered on the list led them once again outside the facility toward the old structures set apart from the newer military ones. The pardoned prisoner they looked for was not housed in the complex.

It was evident by the design that the surrounding grounds came before the Federation. A big wall surrounded a small village. They passed through a front gate, after Rick cut loose an old, rusted lock. Aside from a smashed down trail of footsteps that led from the main gate, under an arch in a second wall, and then to the front entrance of the castle, the rest of the yard still had plant life frozen like sharp spikes from the ground, completely undisturbed.

Cottages were frozen in time and loomed over by an enormous castle. Dark, slick spires rose toward the gray cast sky, just as magnificent as the day they'd been built. Not a single stone looked to be out of place. Evan stopped, taking a deep breath as he peered up. Sturdy, round towers were set into the walls and as they passed under the second, shorter wall, it looked like there might be a walkway overhead.

Seeing a figure near him, stomping forward at a fast pace, he frowned. Something was wrong with Rick. Evan had been getting the smallest glimpses of feeling from the man that was entirely out of character.

"Rick?" Evan asked, drawing the man's attention.

"I'm freezing my balls off. Why in the world would they store prisoners outside the complex?" Rick again trudged forward, moving to catch up to the others. Evan followed behind.

"This place is stranger than a Lipknot on Torgan." Lucien fell into step next to Evan. "It's like time just stopped and the people disappeared."

Evan glanced behind them toward the prison. With all the prisoners dressed the same, he had the feeling the people of this village didn't just disappear. The mystery thickened. Maybe the Federation had been trying to free the people from some strange malady. Maybe the Federation caused the malady. "Dev, what's our reading? Anything out of the ordinary with the environment?"

Dev checked his wrist. "Everything is normal. Why? What are you thinking?"

Evan shook his head, not answering. The truth was, he didn't know.

"Do you think they ran out of room in the prisons and began storing them in the castle?" Viktor asked, his breath coming in soft, white puffs of air.

"These log numbers were the earliest," Rick said. "They were the first prisoners. And the front gates had been sealed shut, locking whoever was at the main complex out."

"Maybe they stored them here as they built the new complex," Jarek said. "And then decided it wasn't worth bothering to move them all since they were protected in this castle fortress."

"I don't think so," Rick answered under his breath.

"What makes you think that?" Evan looked around.

"The dog over there," Rick pointed to the side. They all followed his finger with their eyes. It took a second, but Evan detected the outline of a small creature lying on its stomach under the sheet of ice. "He has the same look about him that the people in the prison had, only he's covered in ice. Something happened here. To all of them."

"Dog?" Lucien asked.

"There, look." Viktor slugged him in the shoulder without real provocation, other than he was cold and looking for ways to aggravate his brother to take his mind off the weather.

"Hey, watch it," Lucien growled, dropping the gear he carried and tackling Viktor. The two rolled around on the ground, hitting the shards of ice that poked up from the moon's surface and destroying them.

"Blessed Stars," Rick yelled, reaching down to pick up the pack. "You can't throw this around like that."

Lucien looked up at Rick from his place in the snow. "Vik can fix it."

"Are you sure? This is from that medical unit. Who knows what kind of technology it is. If we find someone, we'll need what's in this pack in order to thaw them." Rick carried the pack, refusing to give it back when Lucien held out his hand for it.

"What's with you?" Lucien asked. "You're not the only one who hopes we can save someone, but let's face it. The odds of doing any good are slim. At best we can salvage something worth selling for space credits when we stop for fuel."

"Just..." Rick frowned. "Come on. I'm freezing my ass off. This place gives me the creeps."

Evan didn't answer. Rick braced his shoulder against the castle's entryway and pushed. When it didn't move, he reached into Lucien's pack and took out a laser. Aiming it along the frozen seam keeping the door shut, he melted the ice along the entryway, until he was finally able to push through by small degrees.

"All right, we stay in pairs," Jarek ordered. "Put your comms on and leave them on. Dev, sweep for any kind of sensors. I doubt they have warning alarms on this thing, since the complex below didn't, but we don't want to alert the Federation to our nosing around. If you find anything worth scavenging that you can carry, grab it and seal it. If it's too big to seal, leave it behind. We can always bring the ship closer to load, once we've determined we're not bringing some kind of alien virus onboard."

"That's right, space cadets," Jackson barked like a commander, patting his side where the large sample collection kit was. Though initially meant for environmental samples, they found them handy for sealing and storing valuable artifacts. "We didn't borrow this scientific equipment from the ESC for nothing!"

The men laughed, despite the situation, as Rick finally managed to open the door. When Rick turned, Evan saw that he didn't participate in the joking. Through the door, the way was dark, with only narrow streams of light coming through the tall, thin windows.

"Maybe we should have put on masks." Lucien coughed into his hand.

Dev again looked at his wrist. "Air scans are fine."

"We're just being cautious. I highly doubt there is anything dangerous here. Whatever happened here happened a long time ago. That said, my son is on the ship and we're going to be careful." Jarek's explanation wasn't necessary. "Viktor, see what you can do about lights."

Viktor nodded, following Rick inside. He reached to touch along the door frame. Rick made a strange noise and leaned over, running his fingers over the wall. Lights flickered in torch-shaped fixtures along the wall. A few of them didn't light all the way—others sputtered softly, looking as if they might go out completely.

"Lucky guess," Rick said with a light gesture of dismissal.

Evan shared a look with Lucien, who merely shrugged. The men walked into the hall. Dev pushed the door shut, blocking out the cold draft that threatened the castle. Aside from the sun-bleached spots on the dark red carpets where light streamed in from outside, the home was intact. Or at least what Evan would imagine as being intact.

They moved forward, only to come to a large, open room. Rows of tables were set up along the stone floor. A cylinder fireplace in the middle was barren, but it didn't matter. More torch fixtures lit the room. Banners hung on the walls, long strips with images woven inside them. Other, larger cloths formed scenes of men on large animals, swords lifted above their heads.

"Viktor, Lucien," Jarek motioned to the side, indicating they should check the room. "Go back out and check the grounds once you're done in here." The brothers nodded. Dev and Jackson paired up, heading through a side door. To Rick and Evan, the captain said, "Let's check the towers."

"I DON'T THINK there are any prisoners left," Jarek said. "None of the others have found traces of anyone."

"They could have deteriorated, or the logs we found could have been an older copy." Evan's fingers and toes were cold. He unconsciously stretched and bent them in a weak effort to pump warming blood through the stiff digits.

"We keep looking to be sure," Rick said. Evan frowned, part of him wishing he could block Rick's strange mood and another part wanting to explore it to see what was going on inside the pilot.

Evan shared a look with Jarek, but they both nodded in agreement, continuing up the winding stairwell of what they guessed to be the tallest tower. Personal objects of the people who'd lived there decorated the castle. Reaching a cluster of rooms, they entered. Evan found himself alone as they explored, each taking a room but staying within shouting distance. Jarek had been a little more cautious about safety since the birth of his son. The crew understood, even if they were mildly annoyed by it. By the decoration, the area was clearly for the ruler of the castle and his family.

"That's what I'm talking about," Viktor yelled. "We found some treasure."

Evan smiled slightly, tuning out the answering call through their comms. He walked into a private study. This room wasn't like the others. Sickening vibes seemed to snap through the air and his stomach tightened, as if responding to an echoing pain that radiated from the walls. The lights didn't come on, but he could see why instantly in the sunlight coming from outside. Candelabras were overturned, the wax candles broken. The torch fixtures were crushed, hanging from wires on the wall. Furniture had been overturned. Books, their ancient pages weathered to the point they looked as if they'd blow away at the slightest breeze, spilled over the floor.

Something had happened in this room. It wasn't just the out of place destruction, but a feeling, not too unlike the feelings he got when reading someone else. His hands trembled and he realized he was stuck in his place, dread hitting him as something inside him refused to let him turn his head. Forcing his neck to move, he looked directly at the frozen visage of a young woman.

Unlike the other statues, she was intact. Her arms bent at the elbows, lifted up at the side as if she were being held on her feet by unseen hands. Someone spoke through the com, and Evan absently pulled it from his ear, letting it drop on the floor. He couldn't take his eyes away from her, from the sadness he felt when looking directly at her face. His heart beat hard and fast in his chest, drawing him forward on stiff legs. Her eyes were closed, the light coming in from the other room giving contrast to the fine texture of long lashes. Beautiful lips were parted, so full they looked as if she'd been stung by a *raspet*, or worse, beaten. But unlike the other prisoners, she didn't look locked in fear, only sadness.

Evan lifted his hand, hesitating. This woman was a lady, from her long, manicured fingernails to her fine floor-length tunic gown. His fingers hovered along her frail shoulder as it poked out from beneath locks of tousled waist-length wavy hair. The frozen sheen made it impossible to tell what color the locks would be, but they appeared a light brown by the stone's discoloration.

Or was it his imagination? How could he possibly know her hair was brown?

"What happened to you?" he asked, letting his fingers skate lightly over her arm. She was cool to the touch, as hard as the castle that held her in her prison, but he couldn't stop from feeling her. Grainy texture, so fine of a grit, snagged his fingertips in little pulls. Evan closed his eyes, taking a deep breath. He could almost feel the soft flesh, warm and alive, if he imagined it hard enough. Unable to resist, his eyes opened and his gaze dipped to her mouth. The overwhelming need to comfort her washed over him. He began to lean forward, his lids drooping over his eyes as if under a spell.

"Die with honor?" Jarek asked. "Evan, what's with you? Why did you take off your com?"

Evan spun around, his eyes meeting Jarek's. Rick appeared behind the captain. When he moved, Evan must have exposed the woman because both men's eyes rounded.

"Die?" Evan asked, frowning.

"Just now, you said, 'die with honor'," Jarek answered. The tone of his voice changed, making it easy to decipher when he was talking to the group in general through the comms and when he was having a conversation in the room. If everyone really wanted to listen, they could, just as Evan could hear the soft chattering of the others through his unit—at least when he wore his unit.

"When?" Evan found himself glancing back at the woman, only to force his eyes away. The spell, the pull, whatever it was, had broken.

"Just now." Jarek looked past him, eyeing the statue.

"You found one." Rick rushed forward. "Is she intact?"

Rick instantly began running his hands over the woman. Concern rolled through Evan, Rick's concern. Evan took a step back. The rush of feelings he had when seeing her were apparently not uniquely his. It wasn't unusual for a place to remember times of great pain. He'd had sensations of it before—at old massacre sites or towns whose population had been ravaged by yellow plague.

"She's whole." Rick let go of her. "I think we can save her."

"That's right, we found one," Jarek said, clearly speaking into the com. He leaned over, picking up Evan's discarded communicator. Handing it to Evan, he glanced around the room. "This might sound strange, but parts of the palace remind me of the Draig palace back home. Curious how two completely different cultures can design close to the same structures."

"She's the prisoner we've been looking for. See here, her number matches. Two, two, five." Rick picked up a metal plate up off the floor, wiping at it.

"Let me see," Evan reached for the marker, unnecessarily reading it before handing it over to Jarek.

"A treasury filled with jewels and one damsel to rescue," Rick said to the group at large. "I have to say this has been a worthwhile trip."

"Uh, captain," Jackson's voice sounded over the com as Evan slipped it over his head, fitting it into his ear. "I think you should come down here."

"What is it?" Jarek asked.

"A body dump," Dev answered. "Someone threw about fifteen or so bodies into a pit and covered it up. From the tears in the clothing and breaks of the bones, I'd say there was a massacre here. Not everyone in the castle was frozen."

"Either that," Jackson's voice added, "or the rumors of them being thawed and tortured are true."

"There is nothing we can do for them now," Jarek said. "Let's concentrate on getting this woman—"

"Wait, the prisoner is a woman?" Lucien's voice called.

"Kiss my comet, a woman," Viktor added. "I'd call that a successful salvage indeed!"

"Easy with my future wife, captain," Lucien said. "Hold that rock, Rick, is she pretty?"

"Beautiful." Rick's voice was a little breathy.

Evan's gut tightened. Something had been off with Rick and now, as they stood by the woman, the odd feelings only deepened.

Needing to busy himself with work, Evan reached to take the pack from Rick's shoulder. They'd taken the equipment from the prison complex and it contained everything they needed to thaw the woman.

"How heavy?" Jarek asked. "I'd rather do this on the ship by the medical unit."

Rick wrapped his arms around her and tried to lift. "No chance of lifting her out of here like this, especially with that stairwell. It's probably the reason she was left in here."

"If they defrosted the prisoners one by one, it's possible they started below and worked their way up. She's about as far as you can get from the hall below. It could be what saved her life," Jarek said quietly so as not to be heard through the com.

"I wonder why they froze her here if they weren't going to be able to get her out," Rick mused.

"It might not have been planned out," Evan answered. They were all throwing out theories, but they didn't know any of it for sure.

"There is only one way to find out," Jarek said. "We thaw her." Then into the com he ordered, "Vik, get outside and hail the ship. We don't need them right on top of us, but near that front gate so we don't have to run too far. Have Mei get the medical booth ready for a full scan, so all we have to do is put this young lady in there. Also tell Mei to quarantine herself and Parker in our quarters until I know it's safe."

"Do you have a hand-held medic unit?" Evan asked, not really directing the question at either man in particular. "If we do this here, we'll need to stabilize her."

"Um, not to be the space cadet," Lucien said through the com, "but what about all this treasure?"

"We'll come back down for it so the ship doesn't freeze up," Jarek said.

"Can't," Rick answered. "Not enough fuel reserves to land and take off another two times. We'll have to come back, otherwise we'll be floating into a space dock on fumes—if we're lucky."

There was no debate amongst them as to which they would take first—the woman or the treasure. Jarek nodded. "Then we come back. Viktor, Lucien, seal up whatever you can carry that might fetch a good price and then block the treasure the best you can. I doubt anyone will come down here looking, but it can't hurt to be safe and guard our find. Dev and Jackson, finish your search and get whatever you can. I'm going to see what I can find out about the family who lived here. Call me when you're ready to do this." Jarek left to finish searching the rest of the tower.

"The process should be simple." Evan tried not to look at the woman, but found himself staring up at her face. Every nerve pulled him toward her, but before he could act, Rick had his hand on her cheek. Evan cleared his throat, trying to focus. What he felt wasn't his own feelings, they were Rick's. The concern beating in his heart was not his concern. The protectiveness was not his. The fear and the worry were not his. He was channeling Rick, maybe not just Rick but others. His empathic powers had never been so strong.

"We'll get you out of here, star beam, I promise," Rick whispered, saying the words that had been on Evan's tongue.

Evan stood, holding two containers. "The manual says when we combine these two powders, they'll have some kind of chemical reaction and reverse this process. Look in the pack. There should be some injectors. Get them ready."

"This is going to hurt," Rick paused, looking at Evan, "isn't it?"

Evan glanced at the containers, lifting the first and sprinkling a pale green substance over her head. Then, taking the second, he coated the green with pink. When he was done and the statue didn't move, he frowned. "This can't be right. It's too simple."

Very slowly, a light smoke curled from the woman's lips. It danced in the air, as if burning a silent trail along the plump flesh. A pale red burned into the ashen dust of her face, as if coming to life as they watched. The process was slow, but the tip of her nose paled where the smoke hit it. Suddenly, the smoke disappeared up her nostrils, as if being breathed in. The flesh renewed itself faster, her cheeks blooming with rose, as the chemical reaction of the powders burned a trail over her face. More smoke lit the air and Evan tried not to breathe too deeply. It wasn't hard as the breath was caught in his chest. Her hair shimmered at the roots, sparkling down the full wavy light brown length, revealing blonde highlights into its depths. As the growth worked its way down, she coughed.

"It's working," Rick whispered, moving as if to touch her.

Evan swallowed, his gut tight. He stared at her face, waiting for her to open her eyes. His heart beat erratically and he couldn't tell where his feelings ended and Rick's started.

"...*quod intereo per veneration,*" a soft whisper filtered past her lips.

Evan stepped toward her. Rick's shoulder bumped his, but he didn't care. He turned his head to the side, trying to hear her.

"She's speaking, that's a good sign," Rick said. "Right?"

Evan couldn't answer.

"*Ago pugna quod intereo per veneration,*" she whispered again.

Her blue and cream gown was two parts. The blue overtunic was edged with lighter embroidery and had wide sleeves that only went to her elbows. Her cream-colored undertunic hugged tight at the wrists, showing along with the bottom hem of the skirt from beneath the overtunic. A rounded neckline fit across her breasts, exposing the tops of them to view. Evan swallowed, his body tightening more, only this time not in fear but desire. The bodice was snug, fitted tight down to her hips, showing every feminine curve to perfection. The skirt swung out over her slender hips to rest just above her ankles. She was so frail and he knew if he touched her renewing flesh it would be soft and warm. A quiver worked over her as the smoke went down her dress.

"*Ago pugna*—" Suddenly, her words stopped. Her eyes opened and the wide, blue-grey orbs stared directly through him. For a moment, he felt only her. There was sorrow and rage, ripping at his soul and tearing at his heart. Beneath that anger was a sense of betrayal and defeat. His stomach hurt, nausea unsettling him. And then sharp, agonizing pain stabbed his ribs and shoulder. That's when he saw beyond her beauty, to the bruises growing over her eyes and cheek. Scratches opened along her neck, a deep, angry welt, as if it had lain dormant with her body, just waiting for its chance to seep. Blood marred one palm, completely covering her fingers, almost glossy as if it would still be wet to the touch. Her gown was ripped, torn as if she'd struggled before being put into her prison. The woman took a deep breath, a high-pitched sound wheezing from her throat.

"The shot," Evan demanded, fumbling for Rick's hand. The pain was intense and he knew he was connected to her. He'd dropped his guard, let too much of her in. It hurt to breathe. He couldn't grab the shot away from his friend, so instead, ordered, "Give her the injection now."

The woman's mouth opened wider and he was sure she was going to scream. How could she not? There was so much heartache and pain. Her arms stayed locked, as if held. Instead, she blinked, her blue-grey eyes still staring through him, as she said, "Do it, Jack. I'm not afraid of death."

Jack? Did she mean Jackson? Something told Evan she was speaking of someone else, someone the rest of them couldn't see.

Rick put the metal unit to her arm, pressing a button. She jerked as the needle entered her flesh. Evan knew because he felt it, too.

Her eyes cleared for the briefest of moments and Evan knew she saw him. Confusion rushed into him before her whole body weakened and she collapsed forward into Rick's arms.

Evan couldn't move. Her lingering feelings stayed inside of him, as if they were his own. He finally managed a deep breath and then another until all that sounded from his throat was ragged, panting gasps for air. Betrayal. Defeat. Anguish. Disgust. Pain. Pride. Honor. Acceptance. Death. He shook his head, trying to force the feelings out. They weren't his to feel. He didn't want them and yet he didn't want her to take them back. He spent so much of his energies blocking people out, not letting them in too deep, and not daring to go too deeply into them. But this woman broke his guard. She felt too much and Evan knew he'd read too many of her emotions. And, just like Captain Samantha, just like his long dead sister, it would be so very hard to get her out.

CHAPTER 5

Josselyn had a vague sense of being carried, of being wrapped in a musty coverlet, of unbearable cold, of amazing warmth, of tender hands on her body, of a strangely accented voice inside her mind telling her to relax, to not fight, to be careful lest she injure herself more.

More? How could she injure herself more? And what had happened to Jack? To the men who held her? Did the others send a rescue party? But they were late. Too late. Everyone was gone, her brothers, her father, all dead. She would have wept if her eyes weren't already filled with tears of pain.

"Easy. Careful not to jostle her...badly hurt," the soft voice said, more like a thought than a whisper. Though she could translate enough of the star language dialect they used, it was not her native tongue and not a language she used often. It was a universal language known by almost all planets within the charted universes. Her father had insisted they learn it as children, so that they may always speak to traveling dignitaries.

As the ruling family...

Josselyn moaned as her body was hefted and adjusted. Her mind grasped to random images, trying to remember what her father, Lord Craven, had said. His voice was as clear as the summer morning inside her mind. What he said about family?

Honor. Duty. Family. People.

They were random words, words that had meaning but whose sentences she could not put together. What had her father said to them? It seemed important. She couldn't forget, never forget. Josselyn struggled, but the words swam around, unable to be caught.

"Don't die. Blessed Stars, we did something wrong," the voice whispered. It seemed to be getting louder, calling her back from her wandering thoughts.

She remembered the gun in Jack's hand. Did he shoot her? Did these men stop him?

The movement stopped, and she felt as if she were propped up, standing tall even as her ribs throbbed and a trickle of blood ran along her neck from the wound on her throat. Thin lines of warmth danced along her flesh, drawing strange, random trails over her chilled skin. It found her ribs, concentrating its heat, and with each passing moment her breathing became easier. When she could no longer feel but an echo of pain in her side, the heat moved onto her shoulder and she heard a great 'pop'. And so it went, from injury to injury, spreading its blessed numbness over her.

What was it her father had said?

As the ruling family...

Josselyn moaned. She just couldn't remember.

CHAPTER 6

EVAN FROWNED, his feet kicked up as he stared thoughtfully at the control panel to the medical booth. Hours had passed, but the woman was still asleep in the booth. He made sure of it by monitoring her life functions on the console and injecting her with a sleep aid every time she would start to wake up. The room was small, only allowing enough space for the medical booth, the adjoined console, and a couple chairs. The woman was sandwiched between two thick sides that made up the booth. They molded around her form as the machine ran a full diagnostic of her body. Technically, a full scan was rarely used, but Evan wanted to be sure she was all right. Plus, it did a full chemical breakdown of her species.

She was human. Pure, unaltered human. No strands of alien blood. No supernatural subspecies of humanoid. No apparent magical powers. No virus or illnesses. Not even an allergy. Just pure blooded human. But what he couldn't gather is what the Federation wanted imprisoning a colony of humans. For if she was human, odds were the rest of the prisoners were as well. Humans weren't exactly the most threatening race in the known galaxies.

They weren't supposed to have the technology to do a specific species analysis, beyond what the unit needed to work. Such things were regulated and only authorized onboard the main Medical Alliance for Planetary Health ships. The MAPH was just a not-so-clever front for the Medical Mafia. Not so clever because it was pretty much common knowledge amongst anyone who traveled off their home planet, and didn't have their head firmly shoved up the business end of a *glarpenkot*.

Absently pressing a series of buttons on the console screen, he filed her health reports into the ship's main computer for reference and urged the tests to continue. The rest of the crew had spread out after getting her onboard. Rick flew the ship toward the nearest safe space port for fuel. The captain rested with his wife and son in their quarters. Dev and Jackson were back in the VR training room. Lucien and Viktor were probably somewhere arguing over who would be the future Mr. Rescued Woman, or at least her lover. And Lochlann was most likely hiding out in his room after listening to Mei complain about being left behind, though Evan knew for a fact she preferred staying with her son on the ship. The protest was just to assert her strength and keep Jarek on his toes, so he didn't get too over-protective and bossy.

Evan slowly stood, walking toward the medical booth. The tight black of his jumpsuit fit like a second skin. He hadn't taken time to change out of the under-suit after they boarded the ship. As he looked at the woman, he wished he'd thought to put on something a little less revealing of his mood. The unmistakable arousal he felt for her threatened to press from his hips.

Already, her face looked better. Though still full, her lips were not so swollen. The bruises had faded to a yellow-green and would soon go away. He knew from the first moment that she was beautiful, but as the medical laser cleaned the blood from her skin, it left behind creamy flesh, wine-pink lips and long, shiny waves of brown hair. A beautiful woman on a ship full of sexually deprived males? She had nothing to fear, besides endless proposals and flirtations, but her presence would create tension, and tension made crewmen irritable.

Evan suppressed a groan. Already he could feel the tension winding its way down his chest, tightening his stomach and stirring the rod between his thighs to full attention. If he was already so aroused by her, what would happen when she looked at him? When she spoke?

Then he remembered Rick's reaction. Could it be he felt Rick's feelings for the woman? Feelings that were very uncharacteristic for his friend. Or was it that she'd sneaked inside him so he had no choice but to feel protective of her? He knew too much of her emotions.

And then all thoughts left him as a soft whisper of a moan filtered past her lips. Evan tensed, his hand reaching behind him as if to push the button to keep her asleep. He was too far from the console and his hand hit air. The rest of his body didn't follow and he merely stood, staring, breathless and waiting. He wasn't sure how much time had passed before her lashes fluttered. Blue-grey eyes stared at him, the color of the Storm Seas on the water planet of Palpaton.

She blinked several times, her lips parting even as lasers caressed her cheek, mending the last of the bruises and leaving perfect rose and cream flesh in its wake. Words whispered, slipping out of her mouth, but they weren't in any star language he recognized.

"I can't understand," Evan told her.

"As the," she hesitated, her words changing into the universal language he could recognize, "ruling family..."

When she didn't continue, he leaned closer, trying to feel what she was going to say.

"I cannot remember," she finished, her voice exuding overwhelming sadness, as if everything she was hinged on the lost thought.

"You don't have to remember," Evan said. "It's all right. The memory will return."

She blinked, moisture gathering in her blue-grey eyes. Then, a chilly calm came over her emotions. When she spoke again, her words were clear and unhalting as she continued to speak in the universal star language, even as some of her pronunciation seemed antiquated. "I am Lady Josselyn of the House of Craven and I would appreciate someone getting me out of this contraption."

He searched her, trying to feel fear, the force behind the brave front.

"Afterwards, I would speak with your commanding officer. There has been a grave injustice and my mother, Lady Craven, must be warned before harm befalls her." Though she was physically trapped within the medical unit, Evan had the impression she could command a whole planet with just the tone of her voice.

Ah, there it was. Her fear. He found it deep, a small grain bound so tight he doubted Josselyn even knew it was there inside her waiting to unfurl.

Then the truth struck him. She didn't know about the stone prison she'd been in.

"What happened at the castle?" he asked.

Her chin lifted. "What ship is this?"

"*The Conqueror.*"

"And who is your allegiance to?"

Evan considered the question. Somehow, saying they owed allegiance only to themselves seemed too crass. Then, thinking of the captain's family, he said, "The planet of Qurilixen, home of the Var race."

"You are not a governmental ship?"

"We are," again he hesitated, trying to sense her and the best way to answer, "connected to the royal Var family."

"I don't know this race. Are they of the Federation?"

"No." Behind him, the console beeped. She stiffened and he thought it best to treat her according to the apparent station she was used to. "You're in a medical unit, my lady. When the lasers are finished working, it will open and you can step out. Inside, lasers are—"

"I've read about these." Josselyn glanced down.

"My father..." Her eyes drifted slowly up to his. "My father and brothers? Did you find them? There might still be time. If you have this unit…"

Evan shook his head. "It is way past the time for saving anyone. I'm sorry. You are the only one we found."

He expected her to cry. Instead, she swallowed hard, closed her eyes and nodded once. "I knew as much. I did. I need to speak with your commander. I must intercept my mother's ship. There isn't much time. She's to arrive back—"

"My lady, time has passed since you—"

"How long have I been in here?" Josselyn demanded. "A day? Week? How long since you rescued me? Have you had contact with my mother's ship? Does she know what happened? Does she know they're all...? Does she know?"

Evan didn't know how to answer her question. The unit beeped again and he went to it. His hand shaking as he felt the desperation within her start to spread, he pushed a button. She was still asking questions when the booth injected her, forcing her back to sleep. How could he answer her questions? They'd found old bones piled in the castle. Whatever had happened, there was nothing they could do to stop it.

"I thought I heard talking." Jarek came around

the corner. He glanced at Josselyn. "The computer told me her scan was done."

"It is."

"Then why is she still unconscious?" Jarek frowned.

"She doesn't know what time she's in." Evan opened the medical booth manually, catching her as her body drooped. "Her scans are clean. She'll be fine. There's nothing but human in her blood."

"Does she know what happened?" Jarek stood aside as Evan lifted her slight body into his arms. Her gown was torn, but still covered what it needed to.

"Something horrific, I discovered that much. I think those bones we found might have been her family. Brothers and a father from the sound of it." Without thought, Evan walked her toward his own quarters, carrying her through the long metal corridor. The intermediate bands of light they passed under illuminated her face. "She asked to speak to you so we could go and rescue her mother. Lady Josselyn doesn't even know she was imprisoned. She thinks we rescued her from whatever was happening at the time of her incarceration."

"Lady Josselyn?" Jarek arched a brow.

"Her name," Evan took a deep breath. He needed distance from her. Too much of her emotions clouded him, causing compassion and desire where he wasn't sure it would be otherwise. Even unconscious, she invaded him. Well, desire, sure. He wasn't dead. And compassion? He wasn't a monster. Compassion wasn't hard, but the level he felt reminded him of his sister and of Samantha. "Lady Josselyn of the House of Craven."

"Like the family crest we saw." Jarek eyed the woman, lifting her hand from where it hung toward the floor. He swiped a finger over her palm before setting it on her stomach. "It was probably her home we found her in. It makes sense. She looks like a lady. Her hand is smooth, not like you'd expect from anyone else in such a place as the village we found her in. It was a farming community, to be sure. You didn't have the machine correct any scar tissue or calluses, did you?"

"No. Cuts, bruises, broken ribs and a toe, dislocated shoulder, a deeply ripped fingernail, nothing else really to mention." Evan pulled the woman closer.

"You read her, didn't you?" Jarek sighed. "I'm assuming that is why she is unconscious right now. Anything I need to know?"

"She's not a danger to anyone on this ship," Evan assured him, stopping at his door. Running his hand over the wall, he activated the sensor, causing the door to slide up and open. "She has been through a lot, but she is tough."

Jarek glanced inside Evan's room and chuckled to himself.

"What is that look for?" Evan asked, defensively.

"You're the psychic." Jarek laughed harder, as he walked away. "You tell me."

CHAPTER 7

'As the ruling family, it is our duty to sacrifice ourselves for our people. We must protect them from this atrocity. We must fight the evil forces that infiltrate our government. These new laws they try to pass are about money, land and power. So help us all if the alliance with the Federation is signed. It's about the Florencian government taking power from the individual moons, and offering shiny objects to get people to go along. Be assured they have moles in our very homes, politicians and liars who will try to sway votes. As the ruling family, we must fight back in secret when and however we can. We must rebel until the day comes when we can make our true selves known!'

Lady Josselyn opened her eyes, the sound of her father's voice fading. She was not surprised to see the metal grate of the spaceship ceiling above her head. The bed beneath her was firm, more so that the stuffed feather mattress she had in her room. Nor were there birds singing or servants humming to greet her to the day. Her dreams had been of her family, scattered images that faded as she awakened to her new reality. She knew exactly where she was —on a ship called *The Conqueror*. She understood she was with the people who'd rescued her, who healed her. Her mind was clear, no more jumbled thoughts or words.

Pushing up, she wondered if she would see the strange man again watching over her. Somehow, when he was near she'd felt safe. Since the secure feeling was gone, Josselyn knew she was alone.

The chamber was small and rectangular, constructed of metal and lacking in personal touches. In her home, tapestries and portraits covered the walls, as did banners of her family's crest—even in guest rooms. This place had nothing to signify family or home.

A dark grey coverlet spread over the bed like a sheet of cloth-like steel, smooth and flat, adding to the dreary grey theme throughout. The only splash of color was a red quilted blanket across an out-of-place black chair in the corner. A small technolog-ical gadget rested on top. Though they'd chosen to live on a moon with the conveniences of Medieval Earth, each of them had learned of the other times in human history. The device was like nothing she'd ever seen.

Two metal doors, as if molded into the walls, kept her inside. Slowly, she stood from the bed. Her hair spilled over her shoulders and she combed her fingers through it, weaving the long strands at her temples into a braid that coiled around the crown of her head, leaving the back long. She'd done it so many times that it didn't take long.

Her gown had small rips and tears, but nothing could be done for it. Lady Craven always said a person's bearing mattered more than their dress. But then, Josselyn's mother could have been noble in rags.

She wondered if she would again see the man with brown eyes the exact color of medium cream grade Lithorian chocolate. When she woke up in the medical booth, it had been the first thought that struck her as she looked into his eyes. Her favorite chocolate, the ones her mother gave her on her birthday, her one little naughty pleasure when it came to her diet. Silver threaded the short, black hair at his temples. It was dignified and spoke of a commanding presence. A small shiver worked along her spine. She'd never seen such tight clothing on a man before. The black molded over his chest, dipping and rising over the bulge of his muscles.

Josselyn found herself again fussing with her hair and determinedly pulled her hands to her sides. Her back straightened. The shiver was nothing, she assured herself. Just a reaction to the man who'd helped to save her life. But, even as she tried, she couldn't quite recall the other man who'd been standing next to him at the castle. It was all a blurred memory.

There wasn't time for innocent infatuations, nor for displaced affection. She didn't know the man. He didn't know her. It was impossible for there to be anything beyond a physical reaction. Besides, as a lady, society held her to a higher standard when it came to her associations. Her father might be...

Josselyn choked back a wave of pain. She couldn't even think the word. He might not be there with her, but she would make him proud of the lady he raised. As the last surviving Craven, duty fell upon her shoulders and she did not shrink from duty.

Did society's expectations even matter anymore?

Josselyn lifted her chin. Society might not matter, but honoring her family did.

Going to the door on the left, she ran her hand over the seam, not finding a knob or latch. Along the side, a small, square frame was embedded into the metal wall, hardly noticeable. Touching it, she instantly jerked her fingers back as the door slid open. The small room was definitely not the way out. An empty wardrobe, mayhap? What else could the small chamber be used for?

The next door easily slid open as she touched another panel. At least they did not keep her prisoner. Ignoring the thumping in her chest, she refused to let her hands shake as she walked down the shorter length of the metal corridor. A small, etched sign pointed the way. Too bad it wasn't her native language. Taking a breath, she sounded it out, "C-o-ck-p-it. Cock—"

"If that's what you're looking for, star beam," a man said behind her, laughing.

Josselyn turned, her jaw lifting. The man's teasing expression gave the impression that he would say more. Not understanding the joke, she merely gave him a slight smile. "I am Lady Josselyn of the House of Craven. I would speak to your captain, please."

A smirk lined his features and whatever it was he was thinking of saying, he held it back. The way he moved reminded her of some of her father's knights when pretty lady travelers joined them for a banquet. Black, tight pants hugged low on his hips. The crimson, long sleeved shirt snuggly stretched across his chest, the end tucked into his pants. Did all the guys on this ship wear such fitted clothing? They were a stark contrast to the looser long tunics and breeches she was used to seeing on men.

"Have I made a mistake?" Josselyn asked when he didn't answer. "I admit my star languages are rustic. Did you not understand?"

"Your voice is perfect, star beam." The man's easy smile and mischievous expression was very likable. "I had to take a moment to fight my first reaction to introduce myself as your captain."

Josselyn gave a small, surprised laugh at the unhampered honesty.

"In truth, I'm much more important. I'm Rick, the pilot, and I keep us afloat in these here stars." He took another step closer.

Josselyn stiffened, not moving but effectively stopping his advance with her stony expression.

"Hey, no, don't get scared, star beam." Rick held up his hands. "I promise you, no one on this ship is going to hurt you."

"You may address me as 'Lady Josselyn' or 'my lady'," Josselyn corrected.

"But your eyes remind me of a star beam, my lady." Rick's easy smile widened. "Come on, I'll take you to Jarek's quarters." When she didn't move, he said, "The captain, Jarek. You wished to speak to the captain, didn't you? He's with his wife and son. I'm sure Mei will be excited to meet you. You two are the only women onboard."

The man turned and Josselyn followed him back down the corridor toward the end. With nowhere else to look, she found her eyes drifting down his back. Suddenly, he stopped and she quickly diverted her attention to the wall.

"Here we are." Rick knocked against the metal. Seconds later the door slid open.

A slender woman in men's clothing answered, "Rick, what are you doing here? Are our comms on silence? Have you angered another ship by opening your mouth on the transmission waves again?"

"Sorry, no adventure this time. I brought you a friend." Rick motioned to Josselyn.

Mei turned to her.

Josselyn bowed her head in respect. "I am Lady Josselyn of the House of Craven. I requested the audience with Captain Jarek. I must speak with him most urgently about a matter of grave importance. There is a ship we must intercept before it is too late."

A light growl sounded from within the room. The woman chuckled softly.

"I assure you, I am quite serious." Josselyn didn't scream, she never did that, but nor was her tone light. "Lady Craven's ship is about to be attacked. Your help in preventing that will result in untold gratitude from our noble family."

"Lady Craven?" The woman's expression instantly fell. Her brown eyes saddened as she asked, "That was your mother, wasn't it?"

"Was?" Josselyn's knees weakened and she fell to the side. Rick was there, catching her against his chest. Another light growl sounded inside the chamber.

"Bring her in," the woman ordered Rick.

Rick swept Josselyn up into his arms, carrying her inside the captain's quarters. They were larger than the chamber she'd awakened in, but still relatively small compared to her section of the castle. Beautiful yellow and red silk scarves hung along the walls of the open space. Strange flowers danced within their embroidered depths, fluttering as Rick carried her past. On a bed lay a man with long, black hair spilling over his shoulders. Next to him, a baby pumped his arms and legs. The child looked like a tiny version of his father with thick dark waves against his tiny head. Only his eyes appeared more of the woman who answered the door. The man rolled to his feet at their entrance.

"Jarek," the woman said. "This is Lady Josselyn. Lady, this is my husband, Jarek."

Rick still held her in his arms and Josselyn kicked her feet slightly in an effort to get him to set her down.

"Rick," Jarek ordered, pointing to the side. "Put her in the chair."

She half expected the pilot to protest, but he did as he was told. Glad for the chair, Josselyn sank into its thick depths. Rick stood and she waited for him to leave. He didn't.

"You found her ship?" Josselyn eyed the man-dressed woman who was supposedly the lady of the ship. The woman glanced down at the inspection and lightly touched her hips as if embarrassingly examining her own clothes. Josselyn turned her gaze to the captain, her jaw set.

"Mei?" Captain Jarek looked at the woman. The baby on the bed made a gurgling happy noise.

"Lady Josselyn," Mei said. "The time of your mother's ship has passed, long ago. We're not sure what happened on your home moon, but you have been imprisoned for a very long time."

"No," Josselyn shook her head in denial. "I would remember being imprisoned. Florencia's council invaded my home because we opposed their rule over the moons and their alliance with certain Federation factions. The man you saved me from betrayed our family and killed my...killed everyone."

"That might have very well been." Mei's voice was soft, her accent unlike the others. "But you were imprisoned into stone. Someone destroyed your weather satellites and what we guess was a thriving settlement is now a barren moon. I'm sorry to be the one to tell you, but whatever happened to you happened a very long time ago and there is no record of it in any of the public historical databases."

"It happened today," Josselyn whispered. Pain filtered over her, numbing and stabbing at the same time. She closed her eyes as the room spun around her. This couldn't be happening. They were crazy. That was it. They were all mad. "I have heard of no such prisons that will keep a person suspended in time as everything passes. You must be mistaken. Ask the other. He was there. The one with brown eyes. He knows. He saved me. It just happened." Hysteria settled over her and she felt as if her bodice was tightening over her chest. She gasped for breath, her cheeks hot as she looked desperately around the room.

"The Federation had such technology," Jarek assured her. "They've had it for nearly a century from what Viktor and Lucien have discovered. For some reason, they stopped using it."

Josselyn's gaze hardened as she looked at the captain. "We heard Florencia aligned themselves with the Federation, knew our resistance is what prompted the attack, but to use such means to subdue us? Why keep us alive? But, if what you say is true, maybe the others...?"

"No," Jarek shook his head. "You were the only one who could be saved."

What did it matter? If what they said was true,

all was lost. And, if they were crazy, all was still lost. Either way, everything she loved was gone.

"None of this makes sense. I should not be here. Jack had a gun. It was over. We lost." Josselyn wanted to pull at her hair and scratch the memory from her eyes and brain. "I don't believe you. It can't all be gone."

"Rick, why don't you find Evan? I think he might be of service," Mei said. "I'll take her to the commons. Lucien can pull up some of the scouting images we have of the moon."

"All right," Rick agreed.

Mei slipped a hand under her arm, tugging gently. "Perhaps we told you the truth too soon."

Josselyn allowed herself to be pulled to her feet and led away.

None of this is real, she told herself. *None of this is happening. I'm in a dream and when I wake up all will be as it should be.*

CHAPTER 8

EVAN DIDN'T WANT to do this. But, after arguing with Mei for nearly twenty minutes, he'd given up, instinctively knowing she wouldn't relent until he did what she asked. The others wanted him to go to Josselyn, to read her and help her through her grief and confusion. But they didn't know what they asked of him. Her grief and confusion became his until he felt as if he'd lost his family and his home. It reminded him of the loss of his sister—sweet, innocent Evangeline. And, with those feelings, came memories as clear and fresh as the day they happened. He was not blessed with the luxury of forgetting.

Walking into the commons, he stood just inside the doorway. Josselyn's back was to him, her head tilted as she watched the transparent viewing screen floating above the gaming table. The holographic images were of her home moon, barren desolate landscapes, frozen memories of her past.

"If what you say is true," Josselyn's soft voice washed over him, "then I've been imprisoned for a hundred and three years. A whole century has passed by."

Lucien sat next to her. He controlled the viewing screen, showing her landscape photos they'd taken from the air when scouting for a place to land. On her other side, Viktor stood behind Lochlann's chair. Both men appeared uncomfortable, though loath to leave Lady Josselyn. Jackson stayed back, near the couches, watching in silence.

"Here is the prison complex," Lucien said. "This is where we got the powder to free you."

"And where you found the statues of the others?" Josselyn asked, her head not moving as if she couldn't look away from what she saw.

"Yes," Viktor said, quietly. He glanced at Evan, his naturally red-green eyes pleading for his assistance in speaking to the lady. None of them wanted to be the one to tell her bad news. Evan understood why. She looked so delicate. Though, he knew inside she was made of tougher things. A front view of her castle came on screen.

"This is what we found on the ground," Lucien said. "Sorry for all the shaking. The temperatures are pretty harsh on the surface and we were walking at the time. The survey camera is attached to the captain's jacket, so we'll see what he saw."

Josselyn lifted her hand to the transparent image, skimming her finger along the edge of her home. Her touch cut through the floating screen, distorting the picture.

Concerned, Evan stepped into the room, "Lucien, no."

Josselyn turned in her chair, her wide, dry eyes meeting his. He'd expected her to be crying with what she felt. Instead, calmness radiated off her composed features. Without exposing his ability to read her every emotion, and risk scaring her, he couldn't very well voice the objection that she was too upset to see inside her childhood home.

"It's just the castle." Lucien's eyes were wide, trying to pass some hidden meaning to his words as he spoke. Evan's gaze again drifted from Lucien to the noblewoman. "For some reason, the footage of the prison complex is lost. Might have been interference from their electrical system."

Translation: Lucien didn't want the lady to see the crushed stone bodies and either deleted or hid the original footage to spare her.

"Are you sure this is wise?" Evan asked, his words lacking conviction. He couldn't take his eyes from hers. The blue-grey, stormy depths studied him and he felt his heart squeeze. Desire, liquid and hot, struck him hard in the gut. Now that she was mended, it wasn't as easy to temper back the passionate feelings. His eyes narrowed as he looked at her mouth—such full, pretty lips meant for kissing. "The lady has been through much. Perhaps rest would be the best course?"

As the lady's back was turned, Lucien glanced at Josselyn and then the others before shrugging a shoulder to indicate he didn't know.

"I have no need of protection from the truth, sir." Josselyn didn't move, didn't show that she noticed his overzealous attention to her perfect mouth.

Evan began to sweat; worried that the others would see the raging hormones in his expression, notice how his words were stunted as he tried to speak. "I did not mean to imply otherwise, my lady."

"My lady," Lochlann said. "I believe this is one of the remaining crew members you might not have met, Evan Cormier."

"I believe we have." Josselyn stood. "Though, I was a little out of sorts at the time. As I have thanked the others, I should like to thank you for your assistance in freeing me."

Her gown hugged her curves, in what he could only describe as clingingly so. The bodice pulled tight, showcasing the gentle swells of her breasts, gliding down over the shape of her hips. He swallowed. "It was my...duty."

Duty? Had he just said it was his duty? Evan glanced past her, his own idiotic words distracting his overeager brain long enough to look at his friends. They all stared back at him, as if puzzled.

"Oh..." Josselyn's mouth opened, her lips parted to form an oval.

Evan needed to leave before he made a bigger fool of himself. "There aren't any extra rooms on the ship, so you will be staying in my quarters. I'll make room with someone else."

"Not with us," Lucien said. He shared a room with his brother. "We're crowded as is."

"Sorry, cadet," Lochlann laughed. "I need my space."

"And I need my beauty rest," Jackson said. "So I guess the short blast goes to Rick."

Evan tried not to grimace. Bunking with Rick? To Josselyn, he said, "I'll just go remove a few of my things and ready the room for you."

Satisfied he said all the correct things, he nodded curtly and left. Once around the corner, he let loose a long breath, his feet carrying him quickly from the woman's presence. What had just happened? One look into her eyes and he was like a pubescent youth fumbling around a half-naked Galaxy Playmate.

"This ship is too small," he whispered to himself. "I cannot get far enough away."

It took all of Josselyn's inner strength to sit back down and pretend the rude man had no effect whatsoever on her melting insides. Like the other male crewmembers, he dressed in pants so tight they molded his hips. The black material had a dull sheen to its surface. His arms were strong and muscled, like he exercised often. They joined to broad shoulders and a thick chest. The looser material of his short-sleeve, pale brown shirt left his forearms bare. The color of the shirt accented his gaze, making his eyes stand out. They were just as she remembered, deep chocolate pools that she wanted to get lost in.

"I'm sorry for that," Lochlann said. "I've never seen Evan in such a mood. He's normally pretty easygoing."

Great, Josselyn thought wryly, *it was just my presence that put the hard, stone-cast look on his face and the slightly annoyed tone in his voice.*

She tried not to wiggle in her chair. Heated blood pumped through her veins, afflicting her nethers with thoughts she'd rather not have about the brooding chocolate-eyed man. She turned her attention back to the viewing screen, determined to see everything no matter how painful. The image was moving now, leading through an icy version of the village beside her home. Though blurred at points, what they showed her was unmistakable. Everything she knew stood in icy sheets, dusted with fine snow.

"The weather regulating satellite had been blasted," Viktor said. She glanced up at the strange, pale man. His red tinted eyes disconcerted her and she didn't look into them too long. Josselyn nodded. He wasn't saying anything she hadn't been told at least three times.

As the image moved inside the main hall, she stiffened, remembering where her oldest brother lay dying. "Did you find no one else? No evidence of...?"

"There were bones," Lucien said. Viktor made a strange noise. Lucien couldn't meet her gaze.

"I assure you, I would know the full truth." Josselyn said. Though their protectiveness was mildly endearing, it was also highly aggravating. Nothing they said could compare to the memories she tried not to think of in their presence. Such thoughts would only lead to tears and those were best shed in private.

'*Smiles are for the crowd, tears are for the family,*' her mother often said when Josselyn had been frustrated as a child about her station in life. There were many advantages to being noble—servants, power, money and education. But there were sacrifices, as well. Her life was not her own and her actions were watched closely.

"Go on," Josselyn ordered Lucien, using her most regal tone.

"We found bones stacked in a..." Lucien glanced at Viktor.

"I think it might have been a storage hole of some sort," Viktor said.

The images continued playing, showing her around her home as the men had explored. She noticed Evan and Rick stayed with the captain, touching their things, lifting and examining them before setting them back down. The idea that they explored her home like some archeological site they were ready to plunder caused her mouth to tighten. Then again, that's exactly what her home had become.

"How is it no other ships have come to my moon?" Josselyn asked. The camera followed behind Evan and she found herself trying to make out the shape of his backside beneath the puffier snowsuit. "In all this time, no one else found me?"

"No one goes to any of the moons," Lochlann

said. "It's pretty much known as dead space, too far from any viable space ports and a waste of fuel. The odds of a ship straying so far off course are slim."

"So none of the other moons have survived?" Josselyn bit back a tear. How was it everything she knew was gone? Forgotten? An unviable waste of fuel in dead space?

"No," Lochlann and Lucien said at once.

"They are all like yours," Lucien continued.

"Did you check them for prisoners?" she queried.

The men didn't meet her gaze. Lucien said, "There was no time to land on the other moons. We only had fuel enough for the one stop."

The exploration on the viewing screen continued, until finally they had reached her. Since there was no sound, it couldn't be heard what was said. If she had doubts before, they now all faded as she saw her frozen body. The captain's movements made it hard to see exactly what they had done to free her. No one in the commons spoke as the images showed her collapse after she'd been brought back to life.

Lucien stopped the images. "That is all of them. The rest are of us walking back through the castle to the ship. The recorder began to lose power so not much else was captured."

CHAPTER 9

Evan walked around the corner, back into the commons, with a bundle of clothes in his arms. He set them on a chair. Jackson nodded once, but didn't get up from the couch. The others sat just as he'd left them. They were done watching the footage and Josselyn merely glanced his way when he entered.

He had talked himself into some control as he grabbed the change of clothes and tried to make his sparse room presentable for a lady. She'd already seen it and none of the other men's rooms were better suited. He thought about making her a room in the VR Training area, but Jackson and Dev would probably start a gruesome virtual war over her bed in the middle of the night.

"The room is ready if you'd like to be alone, my lady," Evan said.

"Or perhaps food?" Lucien offered. "I'm a wonderful cook."

"You use a food simulator like the rest of us." Jackson shook his head. "The only one on this ship who can cook is Mei."

"That's not true," Lochlann said. "Evan can, in a pinch."

The ship lurched to the side. Josselyn stiffened, her brow drawn in worry as she looked at the others.

"It's probably just Rick dumping fuel," Lucien said in reaction to her startled glance.

"Why would the pilot dump fuel?" Josselyn frowned. She motioned at Lucien. "Didn't you just say there was not enough fuel to explore the other moons?"

Lucien began to open his mouth. Evan stepped forward, stopping the man from mentioning anything about Rick's "pre-arranged" unscheduled pit stops for sex in front of her. "He's joking. Rick would never dump fuel. This is just normal space turbulence found in this part of the sky."

Lucien grinned behind her back.

"I'll take you for food," Evan said, unsure he wanted to leave the flirting dere brothers to entertain her. He recognized the look on Viktor's face and the tone in Lucien's voice. Because they couldn't do anything to cheer her otherwise sad plight, they would start plying her with compliments and not so veiled come-on lines until she either slapped them or took them up on the offers. Either way, she would be distracted. It wasn't the most tactful route to helping a person through a rough time.

Josselyn lifted her hand, as if to take his arm, but Evan was already stepping toward the door. He hadn't meant for his actions to look like a rejection but he could tell that is how she saw it. Her back stiffened and her jaw tilted up. Unable to artfully take back the slight and offer to help her down the hall, he continued forward. He was pretty sure he didn't want her touching him, anyway. If that soft, small hand glided onto his arm, he might not let it stop there. Carrying her unconscious body was one thing, but feeling her willing, mindful touch quite another.

"I thank you for the hospitality of your private chambers," Josselyn said, as if he hadn't rejected her hand. "I hope you will be comfortable in your new accommodations."

"It's not a problem." Evan wished his tone didn't sound so gruff. "I only wish I had better to offer."

"I like that your eyes don't hold pity for me. The others seem at the ready with their handkerchiefs."

Josselyn gave him a slight smile, though sadness filtered in her gaze.

Evan nodded. He did feel for her, not pity per se, but empathy. "Handkerchiefs?"

"It's a little bit of cloth used for wiping tears." Josselyn followed him into the dining hall. Like the rest of the ship, the room was plain. A single, long table stretched along the middle with enough chairs to seat the whole crew. The metal countertop dominated one side, with a food simulator set into the wall above it.

"I'm not sure if you're familiar with the food simulator, but it can materialize about any meal you wish." Evan pressed a button, showing her how to work the machine, as he requested, "Coffee." The simulator dinged and he opened the door. Inside was a steaming white porcelain cup of the bitter, brown liquid. Sam had gotten him used to the human drink. He held it out to Josselyn. "Do you like coffee? I'm told it's a favorite amongst most human cultures."

She took the cup, sniffed, wrinkled her nose and handed it back. "I do not believe I will." Instead, she pushed the button for herself, hesitated, and leaned unnecessarily close to the simulator before stating loudly, "Mead." A low-pitched tone sounded briefly over them.

"It would seem you discovered something the

machine does not know," Evan gave a small laugh. "These are supposed to be programmed for nearly every humanoid life form based food."

She pushed the button again. "Yill." The simulator let off the low tone. Not as loud as before, she asked, "Ale?"

The simulator dinged. Evan opened the door for her, taking out a lukewarm mug of brownish red liquid. The smell of liquor wafted over him. "I should have offered you something stronger. I imagine it can't be easy to discover your world as changed so dramatically."

"Careful." Josselyn took a sip of the ale, only to wrinkle her nose slightly at the taste. It clearly wasn't the flavor she was used to. "Lest I take back what I said about your eyes. Those words almost border on pity."

Evan knew she didn't wish to appear weak, so said nothing about the difference between pity and sympathy. Instead, he looked at her cup. "How is it?"

"Strange," she admitted. Then sighing, she looked around. "It is all so strange."

For a moment, when she looked up at him, her beautiful eyes wide and clear, Evan wished he were more like Rick. He tried to think of something smooth and clever to say to her. Actually, he'd settle for Rick's not so smooth. Trying to remember some of the choice phrases Rick used, he frowned.

Josselyn leaned back. When had she gotten so close? His blood raged with lust. Desire swirled through his thoughts before dancing its way down his stomach to his loins. Images of pressing her up against the counter, her skirts lifted, his pants unbuckled to pool at his feet, entered his mind. He took a deep breath. It was a mistake. The faint smell of her hair, of sweet flowers, wafted over him.

"Can you show me to my chambers?" Her voice soft, she took a step back, putting distance between them. "I was mistaken. I don't think I can eat anything right now."

Evan's frown deepened. Had he been leaning into her, breathing loud and harsh like the maniac he was fast becoming? He adjusted his hips, wishing his pants were looser to let the blood flow to his erection with more ease and glad they weren't because the tight fabric forced the length to stay down.

"Of course, my lady," he managed, potently aware of how close her breasts were to the reach of his hand. He needed to get her into her room before he lost every rational thought in his head and attacked her right here in the dining hall. "You must want rest."

CHAPTER 10

Rest wasn't exactly what she wanted at the moment. Josselyn wondered if his sudden gruffness was because of her obvious advances, or just a natural return of his irritable temperament. For a moment, as he showed her how to get her drink from the machine, he'd softened.

The burn of liquor had trailed a welcome fire down her throat. Josselyn clutched the cup in her hands. She wasn't a fool. Part of her wanted to embrace the insanity of attraction, desperate to feel anything but the pain and loss. Her treacherous body mistook his sudden kindness for attraction. Like a herd of wild horses, desire stampeded its way over her length. Her mind, clearly not wanting to be left out, produced images of his tight pants around his ankles as he trapped her to the countertop and took her hard and fast. The way he pulled away from her, a frown marring his brow, made her think he could read minds and wasn't happy about what was going through hers.

Heat stained her cheeks at the thought. Her gaze traveled down Evan's backside as he walked slightly ahead of her down the corridor. Josselyn had never been taken like that—up against a countertop. She'd seen it done between a servant and a knight one evening after a celebration at the castle. In truth, she'd never been taken up against anything.

It wasn't that she couldn't have lovers. She had lovers over the years. Nothing worth bragging about to the gossiping maids, but they'd been there. Though, both times were really disappointing.

Then why now did these thoughts pervade her when she should be concentrating on other things? Propelled forward by the sound of Evan's steady footfall, she whispered, "I don't want to be awake right now."

"The medic unit can give you something to help you sleep, if you like," Evan offered.

"No, I mean you shouldn't have taken me out of the stone. Not now, not after so long a time has passed. I don't belong here, in this generation or on this ship. Please, take me home. I don't care if the castle is a frozen tundra. It's the only place I have."

Josselyn stopped walking, merely standing in the corridor as she waited for him to look at her.

He didn't but he did stop walking. "If you go back, you will die from the elements."

"I know." Josselyn didn't move. "It's where I belong."

Without warning, Evan spun around to face her, his gaze hard. "You would limp off and die, my lady? Is that how you honor your family? By giving up?"

"Why are you yelling at me?" Her voice cracked, though a deep part of her rose up, taking offense to his words. "I didn't ask you to bring me here."

"We never ask for the bad that happens to us, but it happens. The true test of character is how we go on, what we take from it. If you crawl off and die, what honor do you bestow upon your family's memory?" Evan put his hands on his hips. Then, growling, he ordered, "Come. I'll take you to your chambers."

Josselyn marched angrily after him. How dare he say such things to her? He didn't know her. He knew nothing about her or her family.

"It is easy to speak of things when you do not live them," she charged. "Let us freeze you for a century and you let me know how you feel when you thaw to find everything you know and love gone

—if you even love anything. By your callous tone, I doubt you care for anyone but yourself, at least no one it has pained you to lose."

"You don't know me well enough to speak about my feelings," Evan slid his hand over the wall and the door to the chamber opened. He stood to the side, letting her pass.

"And you are so certain you know me?" she asked. "You think because I am a lady, I will just roll over weakly and die?"

He blinked slowly, as if catching himself. "Didn't you just say that very thing?"

Had she? Josselyn thought back to her words. Yes, she had in a moment of grief thought of crawling off to die in her frozen castle home.

"I might be a lady," Josselyn paused, not sure why she was reaching out to grab him by the shirt. Jerking him into her room, she pulled his face down to hers. The strong urge to kiss him tingled over her lips. She angled her face to his, hissing under her breath, "But I know how to honor my family. If my crawling off to die is what I see fit to do, you will not question my decision."

His face was close now and she didn't readily let go of his shirt. Her fist shook against his chest, as the heat from his breath hit her cheek. The tiny caress sent a shiver over her body.

"There is no honor in choosing death," he said.

"It depends on how you die," she countered.

"What are we arguing about?" His gaze dipped down, as if seeing her close mouth for the first time. "And why?"

"I think you sought to distract me from my grief," Josselyn answered, not sure what made her believe that. "You made me angry on purpose."

"Anger helps." Evan didn't pull away, even as her grip on his shirt weakened. "At least until you find your purpose."

Her tone lightened, the anger leaving as fast as it came. In its wake, a desire to fight settled. "I was wrong about you, wasn't I? You do understand. Is that why you're so angry? You haven't found purpose?"

"I found it." His tone saddened and he drew back, never closing the distance between their lips.

"Who did you lose?" She shivered, feeling cold as his shirt slipped from her fingers.

"A sister. Her name was Evangeline and she was everything pure and good in the universe. She should not have died like she did."

"And your purpose was revenge?" Josselyn understood revenge. She felt it now curling inside her, needing a place to seep out. It was a constant in her rising and falling, churning and twirling emotions. Only, with so much time having passed, who could she seek revenge upon? Was it possible Jack was still alive? He would be a very old man now. Did she seek to destroy any children he might have had? Even if they were innocent of the crimes of their father? And even if her mother survived all of life's tragedies, Lady Craven would have gone on to die of age.

"My purpose was saving Samantha, the daughter of the man who killed my sister," Evan didn't take his eyes off her.

"What happened?" Looking into the brown, steady gaze, Josselyn found herself trying to connect to the man before her. There was something to his ways that reminded her of home and she clung to that feeling.

"Evangeline became sick while we were flying through deep space. There was only the two of us, but we didn't want for anything. We were trying to find a new home world to settle on."

"You said she was killed? Someone poisoned her?"

"Yellow Plague. She helped a man off the ground at a space port. He coughed on her and infected her. We got away before the authorities could activate a quarantine."

"And that man who coughed on her died as well?" Josselyn sat on the bed.

"Yes. Everyone on that planet died. The authorities killed them to stop the plague."

"Then you saved this man's daughter?"

"That was not the man who killed her. That was an accident." Evan began to pace. "We didn't have time to resupply on the port before taking off. Without much option, we were forced to hail Ticaron for help. Gretori Zothos agreed to let us land for an emergency resupply and to help Evangeline. The Ticara are known healers, but they don't usually use their gifts unless it's for their own gain. So I offered to pay him. Apparently, it was not enough. As soon as we landed, Gretori Zothos took us prisoner, locked us in a cell and acquisitioned our ship for his own use. Evangeline died in my arms on a damp, hard cell. Gretori Zothos killed her with his deceit. At least on my ship with the medic unit, she had half a chance."

"And you saved Gretori Zothos's daughter?"

"Samantha. The Ticara cannot heal the dead, though Sam tried. She healed me and nearly killed herself trying to bring back Evangeline. I wasn't sure what to do and was going to leave her where someone could find her and save her, but she begged me to take her away with me and told me how to get to my ship. Later I found out that I stole her from not only her coronation to be princess, where the Ticara take away the complete will of their women, but also her wedding to a man her father chose for her. My ship was to be her bride price to the Ticara lord."

Josselyn didn't move. As he spoke, Evan kept glancing at her, his expression guarded and his tone flat like he talked about the technical makeup of the food simulator. "I saw Federation soldiers led by a betrayer kill my older brothers—Jonathan, Peter and Ralphe—and my father. I did not see the young Rainier die, but was told he fell. My only hope was to find my mother. Now I am alone. No one should have to see a loved one die before their time. I am sorry for your loss." Josselyn blinked, clearing her throat. "What happened to you and Samantha?"

"I sold everything I had, even the ship, so I could watch over Sam. For six months I tended her, hiding from Gretori Zothos' scouts. She recovered and one by one we picked up the rest of our crew. Together we acquisitioned a ship." Evan gave a soft smile. "Actually, Sam won it in a card game from a Kintok."

"A Kintok? The fetishists?" Josselyn looked around the plain room. There were some things everyone in the galaxy seemed to know about, but never discuss, no matter how isolated the planet. The Kintoks being sex traders was one of them. They'd stopped on her moon in their floating brothels and rumors of the things they did on their ships had been whispered into the hall long after they left. Her father would have gone berserk if he had known some of the things her maids told her. She couldn't help it as she looked around the room, trying to see where the chains would come out of the walls, or where the hidden door leading to all the whips would be located.

"A different ship," Evan said.

"Ah," Josselyn gasped in relief. "I mean, of course. I didn't think..."

"Yes, you did." Evan gave a small laugh.

"You were saying, you picked up a crew," she prompted.

"Saved a crew is more like it. Me, Sam, Lucien, Viktor, Rick and Dev."

Josselyn envied this Samantha. The way Evan said her name, with such reverence made her ache to have someone think that fondly of her. "I should like to meet her."

"She's not onboard this ship. She married Captain Jarek's brother and lives the life of a princess."

Josselyn stood, suddenly thinking to understand his pain. Samantha, being a princess, had married according to her rank. Knowing a little something about arranged marriages herself, though never having gone through one, she placed a hand on his arm. He was a stranger to her, yet it seemed natural to try and comfort him.

"What of Dev? Is he with you?"

"Ah, Dev..." He paused. "Dev is a Belvon. Are you familiar with the race?"

Josselyn shook her head in denial.

"He has the look of an Earth culture demon." Evan looked to where her hand touched him. His voice lowered. "He's very large and often scares humanoids."

Josselyn bit the inside of her lip in worry. She had dealt with aliens, but those who looked fairly similar to her. Trying to push her irrational fear aside, she said, "That's nice."

Evan gave her a bemused look. "Dev won't hurt you. I promise."

"Are you offering to place me under your protection?" Josselyn whispered, surprised by the idea.

"If you need it, though I am guessing by your tone that the word protection may have different implications to you than it does to me."

Josselyn frowned. He didn't want her. Not that she could have agreed to such an arrangement. Or could she? It wasn't like she had many options. When they stood close, he could have kissed her. She wasn't sure if it was relief or disappointment she should be feeling. "I want to be alone now."

Evan nodded. He walked to the small, metal room and opened the door. "If you would like to bathe, this is a decontaminator. Run your hand over

126

that wall to activate it. The lasers will do all the work. Mei has offered to find you some clothes, if you like."

Breeches? Like Mei wore? Josselyn's eyes widened.

"Just until we can find something more appropriate at the space port." Evan didn't look at her as he left her alone in the room.

For a moment, Josselyn just sat in silence, staring first at the door from which he left, then at the decontaminator and finally her hands in her lap. Her gaze bore into her fingers, following each detailed line she could find like it was the most important thing in the world. A tear dripped onto her thumb, causing her to jerk violently. The pain she carried was too much and now that she was alone it came tumbling out in a stream of muffled sobs. Her body dropped onto the mattress, shaking uncontrollably. In this moment, trapped on a strange ship, surrounded by strangers, there was nothing to be done.

EVAN STOOD on the other side of the door. He waited for the calmness coming from within to break. Lady Josselyn was very controlled, more than most people he came across. Maybe that is what made him speak of Evangeline to her. He never spoke of his sister, not even to his closest friends. Then why did he tell her? Because she had lost her family? Because she was alone?

Suddenly, a harsh wave of grief broke through the door, bombarding him so hard it felt as if his chest was ripped open. He grabbed his heart, his back sliding against the smooth, metal wall as he stumbled away from her. His own pain over the clear memory of his sister's death, combined with Josselyn's emotions, was too much.

Evan fell to his knees, his hands shaking as he tried to crawl down the corridor. A loud thump sounded and he realized it was his head hitting the floor. His hands shaking, he clutched at his chest, rolling onto his back. Beneath his palms his heart pounded, slamming hard. And then, suddenly, it stopped.

"Evan?" Mei's cry sounded far away in his blackening world. "Evan, what happened? Jarek! *Qing bang-zhu wo, ten nai.* Help! Help..."

CHAPTER 11

EVAN TOUCHED his chest as the beat of his heart quickened. He gripped tight, waiting for the pain to start up again. Two weeks had passed since he collapsed in the corridor and whenever Josselyn came near he worried that her grief over losing all her family would again make his heart stop. No one told her what had happened. Evan didn't want her to know. Not only would it compound her guilt, but there was the risk to his health if she had any more emotional breaks. Besides, for her to discover that being near her had almost killed him would mean she'd discover he had psychic abilities. Life had taught him to be cautious with sharing his gift and he didn't want her to know about that yet.

The few times they had crossed paths, the encounters had been rushed and Evan nearly tripped over himself to get away from her. She seemed comfortable around most of the crew. Only Dev gave her pause, though she tried her best to be as polite to the Belvon as she was to the others. Evan gave Josselyn credit for that much because he felt her nervousness.

"Evan?" Mei asked, her son sleeping in her arms as she rocked him. Since Evan's incident, she'd been hovering around him in worry.

The commons was quiet, except for the soft recording of a Lintianese lullaby drifting sweetly on the still air. The song was meant to make Parker fall asleep, but it worked on Rick, too. The pilot snoozed on the long couch, sprawled out at strange angles, one foot thrown up over the back and the other placed firmly on the floor. His arms bent over his head, framing his slack-jawed features.

"I was just thinking that I should kick Rick out of my bed," Evan said, nodding at the pilot to get Mei to stop scrutinizing his every expression.

Mei chuckled. "I was surprised you even lasted one night sharing a room with him."

Rick snored lightly, adjusting on the couch. He didn't wake up.

"I'm surprised myself," Evan admitted, standing. Walking to the couch, he gently drew Rick's arms down. Rick stayed sleeping, but the angle of his neck shifted enough that the snoring stopped. Evan continued talking to Mei, as he again took his seat. "I much prefer sleeping in the commons than bunking with... What did Rick call himself? The universally renowned instructor of ladies' men? I swear he likes to sit up gabbing like a teenage Shandrot the night before her Announcement Party into Shandronian society."

Mei giggled. "That is bad. We had a shipload of diplomats' daughters land once near my family's palace to buy silk."

Evan's heartbeat lurched and he cleared his throat in response. His body tightened, preparing for Josselyn's appearance. Tension flooded his limbs, causing his whole body to stiffen no matter how relaxed he tried to appear.

"Evan?" Mei's concern was back, as if it had never left. "Are you well? Is it happening again?"

"I'm fine." Evan nodded, not so sure as he looked at the door. Josselyn appeared in the entry-way, her face composed. She wore the same gown they found her in, mended by her own hand. Mei didn't meet Josselyn's gaze as the woman entered. The two didn't have much to say to each other. Evan did his best not to read into it, but knew Mei was hurt by Josselyn's refusal to wear the male style clothing she'd given her. And, oddly, the princess had been seen on several occasions in her fine silk gowns brought with her from her home planet. Mei was too short and slender to share the fine embroidered silk dresses with Josselyn, not that Evan suspected she would have. Today, the Lintianese princess wore tight black pants and a fitted crimson shirt more befitting a member of their crew. Jarek had purchased them for her on a fueling base.

"Can we help you with something, my lady?" Mei asked, stroking her son's cheek. Even though she didn't look at Josselyn, Evan knew Mei's attention was focused on the other woman.

Evan stood, ready to leave.

"Rick offered to take me to the Virtual Reality chamber." Josselyn looked at the sleeping man. "Another time perhaps. I won't disturb him."

"I can show you." Evan wondered why he offered. Josselyn looked at him in surprise.

"Evan, are you sure that's wise?" Mei asked, not getting up from her chair. She adjusted her son in her arms. Josselyn's sharp gaze moved to Mei. "It is only that Dev might be in there with Jackson. If they are fighting, you should not disturb them. Someone could get hurt."

It was an excuse. The "someone" Mei worried about was him.

"Rick made arrangements with Dev," Josselyn said. "They are not there today."

"It is fine, Mei," Evan told her, giving her a meaningful nod to let her know he was all right.

Then to Josselyn, he motioned toward the door. "My lady, shall we?"

Perhaps it was the idea of her spending more time with Rick that caused him to offer to take her. Or that, despite his quickening heart, he wanted to be next to her. He thought about her often, knowing he shouldn't get too close. But today her pain was less than it had been and Evan wanted to be near her.

"Thank you, Evan, for taking me. I need off this ship. I am not used to such close confinement." The strength of her words had grown in confidence as she practiced the star language they all used. "I miss my morning rides through the grassy valleys, watching the sunrise in brilliant magentas, the light growing and dancing."

Evan held his breath, tensing as he waited for her pain to roll inside him.

She sighed heavily. "Did I upset you?"

"No, no," he cleared his throat. "Why would your need for space upset me? It's not uncommon for those fresh to a spaceship to feel—"

"Not that," she gave a small laugh and for the briefest second joy spread throughout him. "You've been avoiding me."

"Have I?" he asked, knowing full and well that he had. Evan patted his chest. "I've been ill."

"Oh, I thought perhaps you were embarrassed

to see me after sharing about your sister." Josselyn stopped walking and placed a gentle hand on his arm. "I can tell you have no wish to speak on it again, but thank you for telling me. It helps knowing I am not the only one who has lost family."

The fingers touching him made the connection between them all the more real and potent. His skin tingled, forcing a jolt of lightening up his arm. He pulled away, unsure what would happen if that lightening reached his heart. The urge to hold her was strong. He wanted the feel of her against him, desired flesh to know flesh, eyes and lips to remain locked as he made love to her like he did in his dreams. Even if she succumbed to him, Evan doubted his health could take her reaching climax.

But, what a way to die...

"Rick is a good man and he likes you." Evan grimaced. Why did he just say that?

"Ah, thanks." Her words were slow and she retracted her hand to her side. "You're not one for small talk, are you? Or for graceful changes in conversation."

"The VR is this way." Evan strode ahead of her, wanting to pound his head into the corridor wall.

Stupid, space cadet. Stupid. Stupid.

What was wrong with him? Here he was somehow babbling and tongue tied at the same time, walking next to the one woman who could kill him with just one bad emotional day, wanting to touch her and all the while trying to find the words to set her interest in *Rick*—of all people!

Rick!

She does seem to spend most of her time with the man, his mind rationalized. *She does seem to enjoy his company and perhaps even understands him when he talks about his twentieth century Old Earth nonsense. Perhaps she is the one to break Rick's part of the Lintianese curse.*

It would be just like a curse to let Rick break it first. Zhang An was probably enjoying this little premonition. Rick, the reason they were all destined to be obsessing and most likely alone, would be the one who found happiness while all his friends were left to rot in misery.

Rick liked Josselyn. That was easy enough to see, even without Evan's empathic powers. He attended her, talked softly and more respectfully to her than any woman Evan had ever seen. If she was the one for Rick, who was he to try and make advances? All he'd get out of the deal was a broken heart—literally.

THIS IS GOING WELL, Joss, Josselyn thought, eyeing the stiff, disagreeable man at her side. *Sacrelue!*

What was his problem? First, he helps to rescue

her, gives her his chambers, and tells her that heart-breaking story about his lost sister and lost love, only to ignore her for two weeks as if she were nothing more than cargo?

Rick assured her that Evan was a kind, gentle, eloquent man. Josselyn resisted the urge to snort. The pilot couldn't be talking about the disastrously brusque man at her side, could he? Or was Evan only cold toward her?

And yet, over the last couple of weeks, as they flew through deep space toward a space port for refueling, she found excuse after excuse to be in his presence—only to watch him find an excuse to leave it. That was why his offer today to take her to the VR chamber had astounded her to the point of near speechlessness.

I should turn my attentions to Rick, she thought. Hate the idea as she did, she knew her situation wasn't the best. The crew on *The Conqueror's* sense of duty toward her would only last for so long. She had no home, no family, no connections and most likely no money if Jack had tortured the treasury's location out of someone in the Craven household. There would come a time when her best option would be to find herself in a man's protection. Maybe that's why Evan appealed to her. He didn't seem to want her, so if he gave her protection it would come at a lower price. Or would that be a higher one since he'd need more convincing?

Sacrelue! That's a lie. I want his protection because I'm attracted to him. There is something about him and it's not just the chocolate eyes or his low, steady voice. It's the chills I get and the way he looks at me when I'm dreaming of him.

If only he'd look at me like that when I was awake.

"I am mad," she whispered, knowing it was true. Only a crazy person would continually put themselves into the path of someone who wished to avoid them.

"Excuse me?" Evan stopped near a door and glanced at her.

"I didn't speak," she lied.

"It is not madness to want to get away from this ship. Whenever you like, you can come here. See that light?" Evan pointed up to the top of the door. "Whenever it is lit, someone is running a program. Otherwise, it's open for use. I recommend sneaking over whenever you see Jackson or Dev in the commons. It's about the only time they give training a rest."

Josselyn followed Evan inside the empty chamber. She didn't get him or his moods. Cold and hot seemed to flow through him like air, ever changing and unpredictable.

White film covered the walls and the space was no larger than the bedchamber she slept in. Her gaze rolled over the length of the small room. Frowning, she said, "Rick indicated I would be able to ride here. There is no room."

"The program can follow you. The floor moves around a track when you walk, so you make it go as far as you like." Evan closed the door.

"But what if two people run in a different direction?" Josselyn looked around, doubtful.

"The program follows each one, changing perception. Though, it does work best if the two stay close." As the door closed, Evan faced her. "These rooms were originally designed for military exercise and training, though Viktor took the violence out of some of the programs. Dev, on the other hand, seems to enjoy putting the violence back in and overriding any safety protocols. Since he's always in here sparring, you'll need to make sure that is the first thing you check." Raising his voice, he said, "Computer, basic control panel."

A transparent screen appeared before them, floating in midair. The navigation appeared simple as he showed her how to reset the controls. When he'd finished, he asked, "Where would you like to go?"

"Some place open, with a warm sun and cool breeze. Maybe the moment when the sun sets along the horizon and colors streak the skies as night falls over the land." Josselyn closed her eyes, almost able to picture the valley beyond her home as if she were there. She swayed lightly, as if caught by the breeze. "Long grasses waving, stirring in random yet perfect patterns over the distance."

A breeze caressed her flesh and Josselyn opened her eyes. The walls glimmered, changing from metal to nature. The scene wasn't what she'd pictured in her head. Instead, an alien landscape spread before her, just as she'd asked. A blue sun shone, warming her flesh and tingling it at the same time, stronger than the artificial light made by the satellite rotating Florencia's Fifth Moon.

The tall, skinny shafts of the surrounding grasses bent stiffly, not swaying like wheat, but instead seeming to fight the wind. Their purple shafts darkened with height until a cotton-like pink fuzz sprouted from the tip, dancing and swirling in a way their lower bases did not. When she reached her hand out to touch the silky tops, the pink withdrew into the shaft like a frightened field mouse into his burrow.

Amazed, she lifted her hand, studying it in the blue light. How pale and cold it looked, almost as if kissed by death yet somehow living. Beyond the field were skinny trees, their branches close to their trunks only to mushroom along the top in an array of spotted jewel colors. Gentle '*pops*' sounded overhead, tiny feet jumping from mushroom tree to mushroom tree.

"Where is this place?" Josselyn asked.

"The VR room," Evan answered. When she lifted an amused brow, he laughed softly. "It was my home planet before war found it and killed off nearly all living things. Now it's a barren wasteland, but this is how it was. I have rarely seen lands so beautiful since."

"Let me see it as it is now," Josselyn said.

Evan hesitated and she was drawn to him, stepping over the soft, bare thatch they stood on overlooking the alien valley.

"Computer," Evan said. "Limpa Valle, present day."

The mushroom trees dripped, withering into brown, ugly clumps of petrified vegetation. Smoke replaced the purple shafts, a constant steam from the cracked, red earth. No longer tinged with sweetness, the air became a stale, hard bite against her lungs.

"You lost everything," she whispered. "Just as I have. Your home burns while mine freezes."

Not knowing what came over her, Josselyn reached to touch him, wanting to be close to him. The ground beneath her feet was hot, akin to lava boiling below the surface—far enough down not to sear her flesh, but close enough to make her toes curl in protest.

"You lost your family, your home..." Josselyn didn't think, as she touched his chest. Heat spread beneath her fingers, pulling her forward with an invisible thread. All around them was destruction and desolation, but the stale air wasn't what made it so hard to breathe. It was Evan, the wavering look in his guarded brown eyes, the sudden part of his lips. She wanted to kiss him, but more than that, she wanted him to want it too.

CHAPTER 12

"You're chilly," Evan said, as he felt the cool touch of her fingers through his shirt. The feel contrasted the heat wafting over them from the VR room. How could she be so cool when his body was on fire? His mind raced for a way to artfully back away from her without making it seem as if he didn't want her. He did want her, badly, but if her sorrow nearly killed him, what would her passion do? Her climax?

He didn't know why he showed her his home planet, the place he remembered from childhood. When she spoke of fields and the sun, it reminded him of home, of a simpler time. But now, in the desolation that had caused him endless pain to look at, he saw her—a bright spot—and the memory of it fell away.

"I don't feel cold," Josselyn said, her voice low and a little breathy.

Would a moment in her arms be worth death? Evan's hand shook as it lifted toward her upturned face. The answer washed over him, a loud cry against the whisper of his rational thoughts.

Yes!

Reason and sanity left him. He felt more of her than he had anyone in a long time. His judgment was clouded. He shouldn't be doing this. If she wasn't in his head he wouldn't be leaning in to kiss her right now. Her need to be close to someone propelled his hands up, fingers hovering along her sides, not touching as he gave her a chance to draw away from him.

Evan moaned lightly as their lips brushed, a small, testing caress. She didn't pull back. How was this possible?

She parted her lips and he deepened the kiss. Aggression built inside him as he gripped her face in his palm. His free hand slid along her hip, pulling her hard against him. The stale air in the VR room made it hard to breathe, or was it the sweet perfume of her hair?

Drawn to the smell, he broke his lips from hers, dragging his mouth along her cheek until his face pressed into her hair. He took a deep breath. "How did you get your hair to smell like this?"

"Food simulator. I had it produce natural ingredients and made my own hair cream." Josselyn's mouth turned toward him, drawing him back into her kiss. "The decontaminator is nice, but leaves a sterile smell when it's finished."

Her soft curves molded along his chest and thighs, cradling his stiff arousal. The beat of his heart picked up speed, but he didn't care. Let the organ explode in his chest. Her engaging taste urged his mouth on. Hands burrowed along his chest, pulling at his shirt. When he withdrew slightly, eager to make sure this is what she really wanted, he was struck by the beauty of her red cast face. Her wide, blue-grey eyes met his boldly and she nodded, as if hearing his unasked question.

"Computer," Evan ground out, his voice hoarse from the mix of his desire and the harshness of the stale air. "Lock the door."

A click sounded, indicating his direction had been followed. It was a programmed noise, not one caused by the actual lock on the door. As he looked at her, he knew this desolate hell was not where he'd take her, but for the life of him, he couldn't think of anywhere else. His mind was blank to all but her. Josselyn pulled on his shirt, freeing it from his pants. Her small, delicate hands slid along his flat stomach.

"This place isn't..." He couldn't concentrate long enough on the thought to get it out at once.

Evan fought the urge to throw her down and lift her skirts. "Not fitting."

Delicate. Lady. Gentle. Go easy. You shouldn't be doing this at all. Unlock the door and leave her. She can't want this. You didn't feel affection for you in her. It's pity that brings her to your arms. Pity and grief and the need to make sense of what happened. She needs to feel something besides loss. Leave her. Don't be her mistake. Don't make her yours.

JOSSELYN PULLED Evan's shirt over his head, trapping his arms. She wasn't sure what came over her. The few times she'd been with anyone, she'd let them take the lead. Somehow she instinctively knew, if left to Evan, he wouldn't make a move. Was it fear of her station that kept him back, even now as she felt his desire pressed against her stomach, tasted it in his kiss, saw it in his eyes?

Other men in her life had feared her station, held it in reverence, let it guide their actions. Was Evan such a man?

Sensing his indecision, even as he allowed her to pull his shirt from his arms, she whispered, "Something soft. A bed."

Nerves bunched her stomach into a tight ball. Would he refuse her? Josselyn looked at his chest, sculpted with perfect muscles, flecked with tiny scars.

"Computer." This time, his words were a mere whisper. "A soft bed in the Var palace on Qurilixen."

The desolation of Limpa Valle dissipated into a large bedchamber. Its smooth stone floor was covered with woven rugs. A large marble fireplace, carved with immaculate detail emitted a soft, orange light. And in the middle, dominating the room, was the bed. The comforter was turned down, showing the dark blue satin sheets beneath the silver coverlet. Two arched doorways led from the room, one with a door and one without.

A knock sounded on the door. Josselyn's eyes widened as she stared at it, instinctively moving away from Evan and their precarious position.

"Someone wants in here?" Josselyn asked. "Those two who like to spar without the safety controls?"

"Dev and Jackson?" Evan asked. Josselyn nodded. "No—"

The door opened. Josselyn reached for his shirt on the floor, tossing it at his chest. He caught it, but merely chuckled.

"My lord," a woman said, entering. The tall, busty brunette looked very real. Her tone dripped with wet sugar. "I've been sent to bring you to the feast in your honor."

"Who is she?" Josselyn asked.

"She's not real." Evan dropped the shirt on the floor. "She's a computer generated image, programmed to react to what we do and say."

"We will be down in a moment," Evan told the woman. "Until then, we wish not to be disturbed."

The woman nodded and left them, closing the door behind her.

Josselyn couldn't take waiting. She went to him, again touching his hot flesh, running her fingers over the taut length of his torso. Her breath caught and she pressed her cheek against his chest, feeling the beat of his heart thumping rapidly against her. Heat radiated from him, making her realize how cold she really was.

Gliding her hands along his sides, she explored his tight stomach and hips, his broad shoulders and muscular arms. Every ounce of her wanted to feel him. The things that held her back in the past with others no longer felt important. She wanted Evan, wanted to feel something other than the pain, and so long as he didn't protest, she was going to take what pleasure she could with him.

She reached her tongue to trace the divot in the center of his chest, licking up until she reached his neck. Sprinkling open-mouth kisses to his ear, she wetted the lobe before blowing gently.

"I wish to be placed under your protection." She allowed her tongue to dance along the rim of his ear. "You are strong and respected by the crew and I am in need of protecting."

"Were you going to ask Rick that today? Is that why you wanted him to bring you here?"

Though his tone was light, she saw the hardness in his expression. Josselyn refused to pull away to see his eyes, afraid he'd read the truth in hers. Yes, she had considered asking Rick, but that wasn't whom she wanted.

"I'm asking you, Evan, not Rick." She took a deep breath. "Rick is kind to me, a real gentleman."

Evan snorted. "Rick? The pilot, Rick?"

"Yes." She frowned. It wasn't a lie. Rick had been a perfect gentleman.

"You're speaking about Rick Hayes? The pilot of our ship?"

Josselyn laughed. "Is it so hard to believe?"

"Only if you know Rick."

"I have only seen a gentleman," she assured Evan. "You yourself told me he was kind. But I would not speak of him. It is you I am asking for protection. I need help discovering what happened to a man named Jack after he betrayed the Craven family. I have to know and the others refuse to talk about it." This time she did pull away, earnestly studying him. "You understand for you have suffered loss. I seek your protection, Evan. Will you give it?"

"I will not let harm befall you, nor will any of the crew." When he moved to pull away, she stopped him. "You do not have to do this. We do not make women exchange virtue for safety on this ship."

"This," she kissed his neck, "is something I want to do. Asking you for protection is something I need to do. What do I know of this time? I do not even know if my noble title holds any weight. And, when we port, not all men will be as honorable as those on this ship. I can defend myself, though having an ally is not only wise, but necessary." Josselyn touched his cheek, turning his face so that her mouth grazed his. "Besides, you've already given me your chambers. Wouldn't you like to move back into them?"

His gaze pierced her as he met her mouth. Josselyn made a soft noise, leaning up so he'd deepen the kiss and give her what she wanted. Desire ran a rampant course through her blood. He didn't make her wait, instantly sweeping his tongue past the barrier of her teeth to take possession of her mouth. She met him without hesitation.

Their tongues mingled, dancing in an erotic rhythm. Her long lashes fluttered over her eyes, blocking out all sight. He tasted of alien wine, not unpleasant but definitely foreign to her mouth. As intriguing as it was, she moved to discover the flavor again and again. The tips of their tongues wound around each other in slow circles.

His hands were on her, rubbing along her back, holding her against him. Her breasts ached to be free and she moved along him to caress her own nipples through the gown. Small pleasure noises escaped her and, everywhere he touched, a fire ignited beneath her flesh. None of the men she'd been with had made her feel this way, so light-headed and giddy. In that moment she knew if she had to seek any man's protection, Evan was the man she wanted most to ask.

Tugging at the laces that held her dress in place at her shoulder, she slipped it from her arm. Suddenly, Evan's hands were there, helping her. Their lips parted, staying close enough that his harsh breath hit her face. He jerked the material down, freeing her breasts as the bodice hung at her waist, trapping her arms in the sleeves at her sides.

Heady with passion, his chocolate eyes stared at her, as if memorizing every detail of her flesh. Her nipples became hard peaks, begging him for atten-tion. Here, in the alien palace, her life seemed even more removed than it did on the ship. Soft blue-green light shone through the open archway, contrasting the firelight that danced over his tanned skin.

Evan took a step forward, and then another, walking her back toward the bed. When the backs of her legs hit the comforter, he stopped. Lowering his head, he drew a tight bud between his lips, biting lightly. Pleasure shot through her, slithering down her chest to rest between her thighs. Without thought, she moaned. Evan bit again, sucking her hard. He cupped her breasts in his hands before releasing the wet, puckered tip from his mouth.

Her arms were trapped along her sides and she pulled trying to free her wrists from her sleeves. Evan's hands slid down her arms, leaving small goosebumps in their wake. With a deft flick, he released her. Now free, her arms seemed to move of their own accord. She grasped him to her, pressing against his firm body, drawing his heat.

Tender, yet insistent, he explored her, gripping and caressing, stroking and kneading. Josselyn pulled at the waistline of his pants, trying to discover how to open them. Automatically, her fingers were at the sides, looking for laces. Not finding them, she muscled him around so that he was turned away from the bed. With a gentle shove, she knocked him onto his back.

The look in his warm eyes made her shiver. He instantly rolled up, grabbing hold of her before she could get the gown pushed off her hips. Josselyn gasped in surprise, as Evan flipped her around onto the mattress. His eyes bore into her, as if searching, even as his hand drew her gown up over her legs, bunching it along her waist. Finally, he smiled. "Ah, there it is. You do want this, don't you?"

Josselyn had a feeling he didn't mean he'd found her wet, naked center so much as something inside her gaze. But whatever he thought to see in her eyes, every part of her focused on the hand that bared her sex. Warm fingers parted her silken folds, forcing them apart. A thumb encircled the swollen pearl buried there and Josselyn ached, panting softly in a primal cry for more.

"So beautiful," he whispered, the sound so light she doubted he knew he spoke. Evan had always been so abrupt around her that this new tone made her shiver in pleasure. "So soft and delicate."

She wasn't the little fragile flower he seemed to think her, but Josselyn didn't protest. Her skirt stayed hiked up around her waist, uncomfortably bunched. She didn't care.

Parting her thighs, she wiggled, causing one of his fingers to slip inside. So little words had passed between them during the course of their acquaintance, yet she felt as if they'd talked every day for years. And yet a big part of her understood he was new to her, that her attraction might be the sinfully sweet look of his brown gaze. Whatever it was, she wanted him like she had no other. Since she opened her eyes, stuck in a strange future world, freed from a stone prison, she had desired him.

"Evan, please," she begged and demanded at the same time. Again she blindly worked at his waistband, tugging it. Then, giving up, she cupped him through the slick black material. The stiff length of his arousal seared her palm. Evan groaned, his hand leaving her sex as he reached behind his back. Soon the material of his pants was free. Josselyn ran her hand around the backside of him, squeezing the rock hard plains of his ass. "I need to feel it. I need your sword to take the pain away."

She rocked her hips into him, working the tight material down along the outside of his thighs. Once free, his shaft sprang forward. Josselyn took him in hand, running her fist over him to mimic what her body wanted to do. She squeezed gently and he quivered. The soft light illuminated his hard features, throwing his muscles into deep contrast.

Evan braced his weight on his arms, angling his hips and pressing forward until she was forced to release her hold. Settling between her legs in one graceful movement, the sudden, hard press of his heat near her sensitive opening caused her to jerk in mild surprise.

Almost instantly, the tip found her wet and ready sex. With a hard jerk, he thrust forward, stretching her tight muscles. The slight pain was well worth the pressure she now felt as he filled her.

"Ah, blessed stars," he groaned. "I didn't realize you'd be so small. I didn't mean to..." Even as he spoke, his hips spasmed, drawing him in and out in a shallow thrust. "Ah, so tight and wet. It's been so long since..." His hips jerked again, the movements stunted as if he tried to stop but couldn't.

"Deeper," Josselyn told him. "Let me feel all of you."

His face contorted in pain, but he obeyed. She made a weak noise of surprise, not realizing just what she'd asked for when she'd begged him to go deep. Her sheathe throbbed, gripping his shaft.

"*Sacrelue,*" she swore. Josselyn rocked her hips, willing him to move.

"I don't wish to—"

"*Sacrelue!* You are not hurting me. Take me already. I am not so delicate I cannot be—" Josselyn's words were cut off by the look of determination and amusement that crossed his sexy features.

Evan withdrew, only to thrust steady and sure. Leaning over, he found the pulse along her throat and kissed it. "Is this what you want, my lady?"

"Yes," she panted. He thrust again, cutting off

anything else she might say. Logic left her and her mind became a blank tapestry.

Rolling his hips in small circles, he moved above her. Josselyn grabbed his face in her palms, kissing him fervently as he pumped inside her. A bolt of longing shot through her as his tongue warred with hers. The torturously precise beat of his hips continued, as Evan pushed his weight back. Her legs wrapped his waist, only to slip down over the backs of his thighs, as the soft bedding caused her to glide up with each thrust. Grinning, Evan followed her before grasping her hip and holding her before him. She loved his smile and found herself wishing he would look at her like that more often.

He growled into her mouth and she answered with a softer moan. One knee slid forward, holding her leg to the side from beneath her thigh. Tension spread throughout her body and he quickened his pace. His expression faded, replaced by one of primitive pleasure.

Josselyn arched, rubbing her stomach and breasts against him, touching everywhere she could. Her eyes opened and closed, catching glimpses of his erotically pleasing muscles working beneath bronzed flesh. Wet fire eased his way and he rode her hard, stroking her to a fevered pitch. The tempo of his hips built—faster, harder, deeper—until her loud cries were joined by his softer grunts.

"Yes," she whispered. *Yes, this is what I want. This. This. Evan.*

EVAN FELT her oncoming climax and fought his own. His heart pounded so hard and fast he worried it might explode. Still, he couldn't stop what was happening. He couldn't resist or deny her. Whatever this lady wanted, she would get from him—even if that meant taking his life. He avoided her for two weeks, two long, agonizing weeks where he could think of little else. This moment should have come as no surprise, not when he felt so connected, so close. Instinct told him she felt him just as deeply, but experience had taught him not to believe such wayward emotions. It was easy to mistake the connection he felt with others as reciprocated when it was not. To her, he was still a stranger.

Josselyn tensed, her mouth widening in a silent scream, as her release ripped through her body. She was so beautiful, so delicate and soft, that merely looking at her left his limbs tingling and numb.

Evan continued to move, helpless against the waves of passion. This was it—the moment of truth, the moment when he could find death in her arms. Suddenly, he too stiffened, frozen above her as his body released into her. A painful surge gripped his chest and he held his breath, waiting for the end even as the pleasure of it washed over him.

Death never came and he was left in the aftermath of pleasure. Relieved and feeling a little silly now the scare was over, he dropped forward, trapping her beneath his larger size. He nuzzled her throat briefly before rolling onto his side. Cradling her to him, he gentle brushed back her hair.

"What does this protection mean?" Evan asked, wondering exactly what it was she asked of him.

Josselyn maneuvered her head onto the crook of his arm, studying his face. Lightly running the tip of her finger over the slope of his nose, she said, "We share a bed, the tasks of daily life. I help you however you need, whether it is physical release or simply to talk. I will keep your house and traditionally manage any servants, though you don't have any. You will protect me from other men, help me to understand this new time." Her fingers skated along his jaw, tracing the folds of his muscles until her hand rested above his skittering heart. Her tone lowered and a wave of seriousness washed over him. "And you help me find Jack. If he's still alive, I will confront him and find a way to extract my vengeance. After, I will give you half of any fortune that has not already been plundered from my home. I'm assuming jewels are still a viable currency."

"Revenge is a hard way to live." Evan covered her hand with his.

"You, better than anyone, should understand I cannot just let it go. He took everything from me. If he is still alive, he should not be allowed to live a moment longer."

And there it was. Her reason. She didn't choose him because she wanted him and only him. She wanted him because she believed he'd help her in her quest for vengeance. She wanted him because he had lost everything. She wanted him because his home was gone.

Locked together in misery.

That wasn't the life Evan wanted. Hesitantly, he said, "It sounds like a marriage."

"Oh, no, not a marriage. When we both agree, or until..."

"Until?"

"Until one of us marries another," she paused. "Then it will be over. No permanent ties beyond what I hope will be a fond friendship."

He didn't want to say yes, not to this, not for her reasons. They were still connected, and, though her grief was there, it was lessened and controlled. Tracing her arm, he moved his fingers over her cool flesh to rest in the valley of her breasts. He closed his eyes, trying to make sense of all the emotions she hid from him. The grief was too strong and new to get past.

"You're not answering," she said.

"I'm thinking."

"Is it because of Samantha?" She didn't move.

Evan's eyes were still closed and he couldn't see her face. Still concentrating on her feelings, he nodded slightly. Yes, Sam had a little something to do about his hesitance. Being emotionally connected to another was hard, especially when every little emotion they had hit his own. It made it impossible to know where he began and they ended and the confusion became something that wasn't real. When you felt so much of another, knew the person's moods, it could be mistaken for love. Only with him and Samantha, they had learned to separate themselves. Sam had known, even before he did, that what they had wasn't true love, but friendship.

"I understand and won't be hurt."

Evan opened his eyes, confused. What was the woman talking about? Thinking it rude to ask her to repeat herself, he said instead, "Yes, if you want it, you have my protection."

What in all the dying stars am I thinking? I am a damn space cadet of a fool.

CHAPTER 13

PROTECTION.

It was what Josselyn asked for and it was what she received. She never realized how bittersweet that one word could be. Now, having secured Evan's pledge, the full realization hit her. And, *oh!*, how her father would mourn this choice for his daughter. It was a good thing Lord Craven didn't live to see her as a 'protected woman'. Though had he lived, she wouldn't have had to seek the security of a man's guardianship. Her father had always had such high hopes that his only daughter would find love and marriage with a man born into high political connections on one of the Florencian moons. Not that he would condemn her for this choice. Lord Craven wasn't like that. He taught his children how to survive and that is all Josselyn was doing. She was surviving long enough to honor her family by finding out what happened to those responsible. This ship and its crew was her only link to the past and she would hold onto it tight.

Protected woman. Josselyn shivered, looking across the commons to where Evan stood talking in low tones to Jarek. "Whore" seemed too crass of a term. "Mistress" was little better.

The men on the ship were kind, but they were still men and flirted endlessly with her. How long before flirtation became something else? No, being Evan's mistress was the best course of action. She would belong to him, safe from all others. It wasn't a wife with a home and family, but it was the best she could manage. And then she realized, she held a small hope inside her heart that someone else had lived, like she had, that they were safe and waiting for her.

"Hey, there, starshine, sorry I couldn't take you to the VR chambers to ride a horse." Rick slid next to her on the couch. "I was busy attending some—"

"Sleep?" Josselyn gave a slight smile. "It's all right. Evan took me."

"Did he?" Rick looked surprised. Amusement filtered through his gaze and she had the strange sense that he was holding back something. She had that feeling a lot with Rick.

"I must tell you. I am under his protection," Josselyn said.

"Oh?" Rick didn't sound too impressed. He nodded absently at Jackson as the man entered arguing with Viktor about the viewing screen in his quarters.

"I swear, Jackson, I didn't erase the movie files to make room for...ah..." Viktor glanced at her. "Other things."

"All the action is gone," Jackson said. "I turned it on to find out what happens to the Old Earth warrior fighting injustice and it is gone."

"He wins," Viktor said, sighing loudly. "In all those movies, the good guy wins. Stuff explodes, they win."

"Well, in your movies the same thing happens. The woman trips, her gown falls off and she says—"

"Hey," Viktor hit Jackson's arm and looked in Josselyn's curious direction.

Jackson frowned, but didn't continue his tirade. "We will discuss this later."

"You're looking well today, my lady," Viktor said to her.

Josselyn smiled at him, nodding once. She turned her attention back to Rick. "I wished to thank you for your kindness."

"Your tone sounds final. Are you going somewhere I should know about? Being the pilot, it might be best if I stop the ship first before you try jumping off." Rick stretched his hands over his head, his feet kicking out before him as he relaxed. The way he acted, especially in front of the others, made it appear as if nothing ever concerned him. If not for a rare, overly serious look he sometimes displayed when staring at her, Josselyn would have thought nothing ever did.

"I've taken Evan's protection," Josselyn said. "He might not like me talking to you. I am told many men get possessive over such things."

"Hey, ah, Ev?" Rick called, not moving from his position on the couch. "Can I talk to your protected lady?"

"Huh?" Evan glanced at them, only to give a flat, "No."

"Thanks." Rick exerted no effort to stand. Josselyn looked at Evan, who in turn continued his conversation with the captain. He didn't come to stop Rick from talking to her. When she again glanced at the pilot, he winked at her, grinning openly. "See, moonbeam, no worries."

Josselyn opened her mouth to speak, but Viktor cut her off. "Protected? By Evan? What's that mean? Don't you mean he's protected from her?"

All eyes turned to Evan.

"What's that mean?" Jackson snickered, as he

repeated Viktor's question. He slugged his friend on the arm, causing Viktor to yelp in exaggerated protest. "If you have to ask, space cadet, you don't need to know and you're definitely too young for the transmissions you've been watching."

"Would you forget about the transmissions already?" Viktor grumped.

"Evan, is this true?" Mei asked from the door, concern in her voice. She had her son cradled on her hip. The boy made light growling noises, very un-baby-like sounds.

Josselyn frowned. Why was Mei so concerned about Evan protecting her?

"Evan, but..." Mei's voice lowered. She turned to her husband. "Jarek?" The woman began speaking rapidly to her husband in her native tongue. Josselyn couldn't make out a single word, but knew that was the point. The soft melody of Mei's voice flowed over the room like a song, but her expression was worried.

"I mean him no harm." Josselyn stood. Why wasn't Evan speaking up? Was it too much to expect him to defend their decision to his crewmates?

"More's the pity for you, Ev." Rick laughed. "Nothing like a little harm in the bedroom, eh?"

"That's protection?" Viktor asked in sudden realization. "Sign me up. How do I get protected?"

"Sorry, friend, but you're not my type." Evan

finally spoke, but it wasn't anything near what Josselyn wanted to hear.

"It's interesting that you are so comfortable announcing this arrangement." Mei directed her hard stare at Josselyn. "Do you make it often?"

Josselyn's jaw tightened. The slight was not lost on her. "No. Not that it is any of your concern, but this would be the first time. However, I was brought up not to hide what I do, but take accountability for it."

"Your first?' Jarek gasped. "Evan, did you know this?"

Josselyn's mouth gaped open and she was sure the blood drained from her face. What Jarek was assuming was not what she meant. And even if it was, it wasn't any of their concern.

"As captain, it is my responsibility to insist that you offer marri—"

"Jarek." To Josselyn's surprise, it was Mei who saved her. The petite woman shook her head once. "No."

"I believe I'll retire." Josselyn walked from the commons, hiding her mortification at the turn the conversation had taken. Growing up in a castle, she was used to everyone knowing her business, but this felt different. These were strangers and they were judging her.

"It's early," Rick protested behind her.

"Mei?" Evan asked. Josselyn's steps slowed, as her ears strained to hear what he would say. But her eavesdropping was interrupted by footsteps coming toward the commons room doorway. Hurrying, she ran down the corridor, her shoes falling lightly against the metal.

EVAN WAITED until Jackson nodded into the room, indicating Josselyn was no longer in the hall. He felt her hurt, but wasn't in a position to do much about it. Turning his attention back to Mei, he said, "You insulted her deeply."

"I didn't mean to." Mei frowned as she read-justed her suddenly active son. Finally giving up, she handed him over to Jarek. The boy tried to claw at his father's chest like a baby kitten, kneading his hands. "But what of your health? It's hard enough keeping you out of her company as it is. If you're her guardian..." Mei's concerned gaze bore into him. "She could kill you, Evan."

Evan thought about making love to her in the VR chamber, of holding her against him afterward. "So could Rick's flying, but I still board the ship before takeoff."

"Eh," Rick protested loudly. "I've only almost

killed us twice this year. And that one time wasn't my fault."

The men laughed. Mei sighed loudly, quirking a bemused brow. Evan was glad to have the attention off his relationship with Josselyn. How could he answer their questions when he didn't have the answers to give? Josselyn came to him because she wanted vengeance. She came for protection. There was so much emotion in her, swirling below the calm surface. Mei was most likely right. Being near Josselyn could literally kill him.

He didn't believe revenge would bring her peace, and yet he still found himself saying to Jarek, "So, what do you think? Should I show her the holo-box pardon we found?"

"If you think it will do her good." Jarek nodded. "I'll leave the decision to you, since it appears she is your ward."

"I think it will do her some good to know people searched for her and tried to pardon her." Evan sighed. "She's lonely and I'm hoping it will take her mind from revenge."

"There is nothing wrong with honoring family," Jarek said. "If it is the right thing, we will help her honor hers. And we must do something. This last week, she's tried asking all of us for help in locating a man named Jack, though we've cut her off before she can even finish saying his name. It is not a conversation we can avoid hearing forever."

Evan knew the captain would offer his services to avenge the Craven family's deaths. It wasn't surprising. Jarek's sense of duty ran deeper than most when it came to family.

"I'm going to go keep Josselyn company," Rick said, starting for the door only to stop and look at Evan. "Unless you forbid it?"

The pilot smirked. Evan shook his head once in denial. "Go on. She seems to enjoy your company whereas we—eh, not-so-much."

"You break my heart." Rick hardly looked wounded as he grabbed his chest and walked out of the room. Yelling from the hall he said, "You know you love being around me. Everyone does!"

"Speaking of broken hearts," Mei inserted. "Are you sure this is wise, Evan? And don't you dare change the subject again, *yung*. I would have my answer."

"Of course it's not wise," Evan answered truthfully. "But it will be all right. If she is with me, she will not be stealing a space pod in the middle of the night to seek revenge on a man who wronged her a hundred years ago."

"Agreed," Jarek said. "Show Josselyn the holo-box before we reach the fueling dock tomorrow.

Give her some hope. Perhaps it will keep her from running away on another ship when we dock."

"I don't think she would," Mei said.

"We don't know that she won't," Jarek answered. His son gave a small gurgling growl and the captain laughed. "There's my fierce little Var. You'll be hunting yorkins with your cousins very soon."

CHAPTER 14

"Josselyn, hold on for a moment."

Josselyn turned at Rick's call. Small lines edged the corner of his mouth. He wasn't happy.

"Taking Evan as your protector was not necessary." As he joined her in the hall, Rick put a gentle hand on her arm. "I would protect you and not demand anything in return."

Josselyn sighed. "You don't approve of my choice?"

"I'm saying you didn't have to make it. Evan will let you out of the agreement if you ask him."

Josselyn shook her head. "I don't want out. I gave my word and would not have myself appear to be of loose morals to the rest of the crew."

"No one would think that," Rick disagreed.

"Yes they would. They are men and I the only

unmarried woman for thousands of space miles."
Josselyn patted his hand before letting her fingers
rest over his touch. "I'm sorry if my decision hurt
you. I never meant to imply there was more
between us."

"You didn't and there isn't." Rick smiled. "I am
not made for one woman, not even one so fine as
you, my lady. My concern is for other reasons."

"You say that, but you never hint at what those
reasons might be." She searched his eyes.

Rick leaned forward, his tone lowering in confidence. "And I probably never will."

EVAN DUCKED BACK BEHIND A CORNER, breathing
hard as the image of Rick and Josselyn burned into
his mind. He saw the intimate touch of Rick's hand,
detected the man's concern and sadness as he whispered to the lady. Josselyn didn't back away and
didn't remove the pilot's hand from her. In fact, she
seemed to be holding him to her.

What was happening? Were his first suspicions
correct? Did Josselyn and Rick belong together?

Even as the memories of their shared passion
washed over him, he couldn't deny the connection
he'd felt between Rick and their liberated prisoner
since the first instant Rick saw her in her stone

prison. They were both human and he'd seen things in Rick since Josselyn's appearance that he'd never seen in the man. Did Rick care for her? Could Rick love her?

Evan refused to think about it. Josselyn was his now. She asked him to protect her and he wasn't eager to let her out of the bargain. The taste of her was too new, the memory of it too arousing. His blood heated with just the idea of touching her again. As his thoughts turned to passion, propelled by the stirring between his hips, Evan found himself again moving around the corner to face the two.

Rick walked toward him, only to nod once as he brushed past. Evan ignored him, instead chasing after the glimpse of skirt he saw rounding another corner toward the private quarters. Each step saw another rational thought slipping from his mind, leaving nothing but pure instinct, the animalistic, primal need to lay claim to what was his.

Where did these thoughts come from? Evan wasn't a tyrant. He wasn't a jealous man. He didn't "claim" things, didn't feel the need to mark women so completely like a Var shifter. And, yet, here he was, speeding each step to catch up to Josselyn.

Already he smelled her, the sweet scent left by her hair. Or was that a memory, so imbedded in his nose that he could breathe nothing else? She penetrated him, body and soul. But he knew she couldn't feel the same way. She didn't feel him like he did her.

His breathing became harsh, almost stalkingly so, as his footfall alerted her to his presence. She gasped, pausing as her hand lifted up over the scanner to open his door.

"Evan, what is it? Did something happen?" She asked, her eyes round with worry. "Why are you looking at me like that? What is it? Are you mad about Rick talk—?"

Her words ended abruptly as he touched her cheek. Cool flesh met his fingers, shocking in its low temperature. Evan didn't care, didn't think on it more than a moment. The door behind her slid open and he didn't stop walking, forcing her back.

"Evan?" she whispered, almost shrinking away from his intensity.

"You do something to me." The words were soft and hoarse, barely audible in the quiet quarters. Her soft skin held his hand to her cheek like a powerful magnet. He couldn't withdraw. "You make me not myself."

Josselyn's beautiful mouth opened as if to answer. The sight was all the provocation Evan needed. He moaned lightly, dipping his head forward to kiss her even as his fingers slipped into her hair, dragging her face toward his.

"I—"

Whatever words she'd offer were lost as he crushed his lips passionately against hers, instantly deepening into an urgent, almost brutal kiss. He needed to feel her, to kill the barren loneliness he felt in his soul. Her emotions clouded him until there wasn't any part of him left that didn't feel her in some way.

Evan said nothing more as he dropped his hand from her hair onto her shoulder, only to slide down to grip her arm. Holding her before him, he made sure there was no chance of escape. The hard length of his member pressed into his tight pants, begging for release. He walked her toward the bed, causing her to stumble. The hold on her arm kept her from falling.

Finally breaking the kiss, he heard her raspy breathing falling hard over the chamber. His eyes burned, his fingers itched. He needed to see and feel flesh against him.

His palms slid along her exposed cleavage and his fingers curled, turning around to dip beneath the dress. Pulling forward on the bodice, he ripped the material. Breasts spilled forth, naked and ripe. Lust shot a path along his entire length, curling his toes, weakening his knees, tightening his stomach and dizzying his mind.

"Ah," the word left him on a breathy whisper. Instantly his palms were on her chest, squeezing them until nipples hardened into peaks between his thumbs and forefingers.

"Ev..." she breathed heavily. Josselyn touched his arms and he realized she'd been holding back.

His head dipped forward and Evan captured a nipple between his lips. He sucked hard, groaning in delight at the hard budded texture surrounded by a softer mound. The sound of ripping material mingled with their panting breaths. He tugged hard, causing her body to jerk against him as he tried to rid her of the gown. The nipple slipped from his mouth.

"I need to taste you." He groaned, his eyes eager to see the damp nipple he left behind.

"But...?" Josselyn looked down at her chest, her brow furrowed in confusion.

"No." Evan let a slow grin curl one corner of his lips. He yanked the torn gown off over her hips. It slid to the floor, pooling at her feet. He gave a meaningful glance to the short thatch of hair between her thighs. "There." Reaching to touch the sexy mound, his tone deepened. "Here."

Josselyn was completely naked, a feast for his eyes, and yet she'd only managed to ruffle his tight shirt. That in itself was an erotic thought. Evan felt powerful and controlling. The long line of her body, exposed to his whims. Full breasts, tapered waist, warm damp curls, strong legs...

"Oh," the word filtered past her lips on a raspy pant. Evan stroked her sex, letting his finger dip between the soft, wet lips. Josselyn held on tight, using his shoulders for support as her legs wobbled.

"Sit on the bed," Evan ordered, walking her until her legs hit the edge of the mattress. She instantly collapsed, sitting on the edge. Without thought, he knelt before her, pushing her thighs apart even as he tugged her hips forward. Josselyn fell back and the cutest soft noises came from her mouth.

Surging forward, he kissed her sex, his tongue instantly exploring the soft petals his fingers had opened. Warm and wet, her intoxicating taste exploded into his mouth. Evan groaned, gripping her legs to keep her pressed tight to his mouth. His tongue lapped, pressing in long hard strokes along her slit. She jerked as he skimmed the hard pearl hidden among the velvet depths. Instantly concentrating his efforts, he sucked hard, moaning loud so that it vibrated against her sensitive flesh.

Josselyn continued to make soft noises, her head thrashing as her arms lifted over her head. Evan reached behind his back, fumbling to undo his pants. Her hips jerked violently as he grazed her clit with his teeth.

He loosened his pants, dipping his hand down into the waistband to touch his arousal as she began to climax. He pumped his fist over the length the best he could. The turgid flesh ached for more, even as he gripped it tighter.

Ah, yeah...

Josselyn arched, giving him a full, underside view of her breasts as he looked up her flushed body. He wanted to devour every inch of her. Evan gripped his balls, rolling them in his palm. His mouth continued to work, exciting an orgasm to rip from inside her.

"Oh, oh, oh," she panted incoherently, over and over.

Her slick, hot center was right there, open and ready. He couldn't resist. Lifting up between her thighs, his arousal still in his palm, he put his knee on the edge of the bed. Her legs flopped weakly, waving back and forth as if she would try to push herself up but couldn't.

With one hand, he pushed his pants down far enough to completely free his shaft. Eager to feel the wet heat of her around him, he guided himself to her opening. She was still soaked from her climax and he slid easily past the folds.

"Yeah," Evan growled, seating himself fully. "Ah, yeah." A satisfied moan sounded, but he was too mindless to know if it was hers or his. He withdrew only to thrust hard. "You do something to me, Josselyn. You make me forget myself."

Her round, perfect eyes seemed to pierce through him. Tremors racked her body, causing her to shiver. Every masculine instinct in him wanted to pound fast and hard, but he held back, instead moving steadily in deep, long thrusts. Their gazes locked and a force bigger than any he'd ever felt took over, joining them completely.

His hips rolled in small circles. The tight squeeze of her body over his shaft, hugging and releasing with each push, felt so damn good he could barely breathe. Her hands brushed his chest, gliding down his sides, glancing over his ribs before curling along his butt. She pulled him toward her, her legs spreading wider as she met his rhythm. Lashes fluttered, as her eyes rolled back.

Evan's heart raced, as if ready to tear out of his chest. Her nearness always did that to him and their shared pleasure only made the condition worse. As his climax neared, he slowed, savoring the last moments. He dropped his head forward, his mouth open as if to kiss her but for the distance between their lips.

Josselyn's head turned, her jaw tilting as she met with release. The quivers of her tight hold over his shaft spurred him to join her and he jerked, not as delicate as she, spilling his seed deep inside her.

Finally allowing his lips to touch hers, he kissed her gently. A satisfied expression crossed his relaxed features, spreading throughout him, only to be contradicted by his racing heart.

"You do something to me," he whispered, breaking the kiss.

"I know, I make you not yourself," she answered just as softly.

CHAPTER 15

"I HAVE SOMETHING TO SHOW YOU." Evan stood beside the bed.

Josselyn watched his naked backside, sated from their lovemaking. His body was all sinew and muscle. Not a measure of fat marred his perfect, smooth frame. His movements weren't refined, not in the way she was used to seeing in nobleman, but they were graceful. But even for that grace, there was a dominating air to the way his muscles rippled beneath the tanned surface of his skin.

"I think you should see it," he continued.

"What is it?" Josselyn forced her eyes from him and reached for her gown. The relaxation of their lovemaking left her as she gasped. The dress was torn. Sitting naked on the bed, she tried frantically to pull the material together. It would be impossible to mend.

"I will replace it," Evan said, his tone apologetic. He crossed to the wall, opening one of the metal drawers. Taking out a clean set of clothing, the same ones Mei had tried to give her, he placed them on the bed. "These will do until we make port. It might be better to hide your feminine curves a bit. This can be a rough place. Unless you would rather stay aboard the ship while we're gone?"

The way he said the words made her shiver. It was as if he could read her thoughts. She was nervous about going on the fueling dock, nervous and excited and scared. Grief had ruled her emotions when she first boarded the ship and by the time she could think straight, she was used to the change from the castle to spaceship. There was an odd security in the familial way the crew interacted with one another. But now, she'd be surrounded by aliens, perhaps even those stranger than Dev in appearance and manners. Her family wasn't there to protect her.

But Evan was.

Josselyn stood beside the bed, grabbing a shirt.

"I want to go." Josselyn, not wishing to be forced to stay behind, quickly asked, "What was it you wanted to show me?"

Evan's eyes roamed down over her naked chest.

His heated perusal caused a blush to warm her cheeks and she quickly slipped the dark blue shirt over her head. Material that would have been tight on Evan hung loosely along her hips, only straining slightly against her breasts. He tilted his head, breathing deeply as his gaze slid down along her hip to where the shirt brushed against the very tops of her thighs.

"You wished to show me something?" Josselyn repeated, clearing her throat lightly to get his attention away from her barely hidden sex and back on her face.

He glanced up, blinking a few times before nodding. "Finish dressing and I'll take you."

Josselyn pulled the black pants over her hips. Threading the belt and looping it as she had back home, so the end fell down in front instead of continuing around the waist like the crewmen's. The strange garb rubbed her thighs as she moved and for a woman raised in dresses she felt incredibly out of sorts. Every other step had her pulling along the hips, trying to adjust what had to be one of the more uncomfortable pieces of clothing she'd ever put on.

She studied Evan from the corner of her eye as they walked. He was different than most men she'd known. Though moody and overly quiet at times, there was something to him that reminded her of herself—like an invisible extension, or perhaps even an extra arm. Josselyn wrinkled her nose. What a strange notion to have? Evan, her new lover, was like an extra appendage?

Reaching to touch his arm, she stiffened.

"...prisoner two, two, five, release order number six, nine, twelve. This is..."

The words stopped. Josselyn recoiled from Evan, making a weak noise. "Jack."

"Josselyn?" Evan turned to her, his hand in the air. She stumbled back, her wide eyes trying to see past the innocence of his chocolate gaze.

"You've been lying to me," she whispered. Guilt filtered over his features and she knew it was true. "I've been a fool to believe you were from the future, coming to rescue me. What is the plan, Evan? What does Jack want? The location of the family fortune? Are you to trick me into talking about the past? Is that your game? Make me believe that everyone I know is dead so I'll say their names and you will be able to arrest them for daring to defy the coalition?"

"Six, nine..." Jack's voice repeated.

"Josselyn," Evan began to shake his head and she could see he was going to deny it. But what was the more plausible truth? That she was held a prisoner in stone, untouched and unknown for over a century? That time had forgotten her and her family? That the Federation blew up their weather satellites, froze her homeland and turned it into a prison complex that no one really knew very much about?

Or that this was all an elaborate scheme to gain her trust and make her accidentally give names of people, of allies she believed dead? The coalition would love to have the names hidden within the depths of her brain. Would they not go to any lengths to make that happen? What about the others?

She had held them, seen their blood and their wounds, felt them die, but what if they hadn't died. What if her family was stuck on other ships being fed the same lies she had been? They could be out there, thinking themselves alone.

It was quite possible they weren't even on a ship, but in a laboratory, and this ship, these people... Josselyn gasped, a loud, high-pitched breath wheezing down her throat. She was betrayed. Her nose burned, as she looked at Evan. How many watched her fall so easily for him?

"Jack," she growled, knowing who was really to blame. Angry, she shot past Evan, pushing him in the arm. He fell out of her way easily, clutching his chest. She found the action overly dramatic considering how hard she shoved him and didn't bother to stop to make sure he was uninjured. "Show yourself, coward. Jack, I know you're..."

Josselyn walked into the dining hall. The crew sat around a table and instantly she detected Jack wasn't with them. Then she saw him or what could be him, as a strange, transparent image standing on a small platform of a box.

"I don't get it? Who are you people?" Josselyn asked, glaring at the little man. Though one of the fanciest communicators she'd ever seen, she wasn't fooled. The transparent image became brighter for a moment. "Jack's father?"

"This is General Stephans of what was *formerly* the Earth Settlement on Florencia's Fifth Moon and this is an—"

"Another trick? I wasn't speaking fast enough so you've decided to add another level to the charade? You think a little bit of makeup and aging is going to fool me?" Josselyn interrupted the man in shiny white. "Where is my mother, Jack? What have you done to her?"

The man didn't move, didn't answer.

"Well?" She demanded. Josselyn turned her attention over the table, marking where each one sat. Dev was gone and her spine tingled to think he could come up behind her. She slowly moved to the side, angling her body so her back wasn't to the door. Rick was also gone and she knew they'd have her believe he was flying the ship.

Mei stared at Josselyn's pants, the woman's eyes

drawn into small slits as she studied the masculine attire. Josselyn resisted the urge to adjust herself. Jarek stood behind his wife's chair, their child nowhere to be seen. Lochlann leaned against the counter, a piece of blue food in his hand as it hovered over a trencher. Lucien and Viktor were near the miniature Jack.

"My lady," Jackson began, pushing up from the table.

Josselyn glared at him, not sparing him an ounce of her wrath. Anger seeped from every pore but instead of feeling hot, she felt cold inside—frozen to the depths.

"Josselyn, where's Evan?" Viktor asked, his tone softer than Jackson's had been. "He asked me to get this ready for you to look at. It's the transmission we found. This is the reason we knew how to release you."

"What?" Josselyn's temper lost some of its fire. They were all looking at her so earnestly. "I don't believe you. I can't..." Her voice cracked, held by the desire to cry out. She'd been so sure that her mother was alive, that she was in the right time, that vengeance was closer than she'd known it to be moments before.

"Watch," Lucien urged her. Viktor reached forward, tapping the round platform. The little figure moved.

"Top secret. Prisoner two, two, five release order number six, nine, twelve. This is General Stephans of the Earth Settlement on Florencia's Fifth Moon." Jack's miniature fingers pushed through his dark hair, a gesture she recognized from when he was worried about something. The fact that she knew him so well only made his betrayal of them all that much worse. His hand fell to the side and the images flickered like dying white torchlight. Jack's mouth was opened, agape.

"That's it?" Josselyn asked, every part of her not wanting to again believe in them. If she believed they were telling the truth, it meant she had to again give up on the hope of seeing her family. She clung to that hope, seizing it inside her cold chest.

"It's old and freezes up. Hold on." Viktor tapped it again, his finger thumping hard against the platform, causing it to flicker.

"...release authorized by my superiors and hereby given to the commanding warden in Ice Complex Five, Authorization code H forty-seven, fifty-one." The sound of Jack's voice, tinted with a hardness even beyond that which she'd known him to carry, made her want to vomit. "When the ice storms came nearly forty years ago, many of my men were killed. It was too cold to stay and finish our work releasing certain political prisoners and we abandoned post on supreme orders. However, there are a few who remain that should not, as they have been pardoned for their crimes. Attached is a list of prisoners set for immediate release. They will be hostile and should be escorted and left on the Rifflen base in the V Quadrant. No provisions beyond those orders are necessary."

"Jack is on Rifflen?" Josselyn whispered. "Where is that?"

"Not far from the fueling dock," Viktor answered.

"Vik," Lucien scolded, as if his brother wasn't supposed to tell her that.

"Hey, Viktor, what's up with the comms?" came Rick's faraway shout. "I've been trying to—*Holy Space Balls*!" The sound of footfall running hard and heavy down the corridor echoed throughout the dining hall. "Evan, blast it, someone help me!"

"What did you do?" Mei charged, glaring at Josselyn, even before she could possibly know the cause of Evan's plight.

Josselyn's heart sunk into the pit of her stomach, as she remembered seeing him fall away from her. "I—"

"Evan?" Mei yelled, before launching into a long, Lintianese tirade that clearly would not translate prettily into Josselyn's language. The petite woman ran out of the dining hall. The others followed. Josselyn didn't move quite so fast.

A commotion of shouted orders, exclamations, and even a few curses flowed over Josselyn as she forced herself to look out of the dining hall, down the corridor where she'd last seen Evan. Rick and Jarek had him hoisted in their arms. His face was pale, his eyes open but lifelessly staring into a fixed distance.

"Is he...?" Josselyn tried to ask, but her words were too soft and the others weren't paying attention to hear them anyway.

Mei glared at her as the others passed, taking Evan down to the medical unit. The woman grabbed Josselyn's arm in a bruising grip and jerked her along. "Come see what you did. And may your ancestors help you if anything happens to him, for no one on this crew will."

"I..." Josselyn didn't fight the woman's rough hold. Too many of her emotions were swirling in her head. "I barely pushed him."

CHAPTER 16

"I WARNED HIM ABOUT YOU." Mei paced the small room that housed the medical booth, deigning to glare in Josselyn's direction for good measure. Josselyn's backside was sore from sitting on the hard ground, but she didn't dare move. It's the place Mei had shoved her to nearly three hours ago and it's the place she remained in as she waited for Evan to wake up. No one would tell her what had happened, only that it was her fault—well, Mei really was the only one saying it was her fault, but the wary looks of the others didn't help soften the blow of the irate woman's words. "I told him bringing a cursed one onto the ship was bad luck."

"Is it my presence on this ship, or the fact that I'm a woman who has his affections that irritates you so much?" Josselyn blinked, surprised that the hard words had slipped past her own lips. But how could they not? Mei had been hurling insults at her head since they entered the room.

"What?" Mei gasped, her mouth wide.

"I see the way you look at me, especially when I'm with him. You don't conceal your thoughts too well. I'm surprised your husband hasn't caught on to your affections for Evan. In my homeland, men do not tolerate such acts from their wives—even when the alliances are made out of politics and not love."

"I love my husband," Mei defended, as if completely shocked that anyone could assume otherwise.

"A surprise to even him, I'd wager," Josselyn mumbled, staring at the corner of the medical booth. She couldn't bring herself to look at Evan's pale face.

"How dare you speak to me like that? I am a Lintianese princess, raised in honor and bound by my words and my deeds to my husband in love." Mei tilted her chin regally in the air.

"And I am Lady Josselyn of the noble House of Craven, raised in true honor and title, bred to know my duty to my family and I would not make eyes at a man while bound to another." Josselyn pushed against the wall, her legs stinging as she made them support her weight. She was almost sorry for the change in position, as it gave her a full view of Evan trapped inside the medical contraption. He hadn't moved since they put him in.

"I don't 'make eyes' at any man but my husband!" Mei argued. "I love him."

"You keep saying it," Josselyn said. "But your actions do not show it."

"What do you know of my actions? All you think of is yourself. Why else would you not see the effect you have on him?" Mei pointed at Evan. "You are killing him. We all see it. Evan feels it. But you, who think to care for him intimately enough to call him lover, don't even understand what you do. All you see is a means to protect yourself."

"You have judged me since I came aboard this ship," Josselyn accused.

"As you have me," Mei countered.

Josselyn frowned. It was true. Since the first moment she glanced at the supposed princess in her male attire, she'd made assumptions. Not all impressions were wrong. Looking at Evan, his unmoving body, she shivered. "How am I killing him? Why is this my fault?"

"So you do see it. You feel it." Mei sounded smug and Josselyn didn't appreciate the tone.

A coldness worked up Josselyn's spine, as if someone shoved icy fingers between the bones and wouldn't take them back out. From there, her nerves stung, the cold prickling and spreading throughout her body like frost streaking over glass. Mei's expression didn't change and Josselyn was compelled to insist. "How am I killing him?"

"He's empathic," Mei said, finally taking her piercing gaze away. The woman looked at Evan. "He feels what we feel and your emotions—your doubt, your grief, your pain..." Mei sighed.

"He feels what I feel?" Josselyn didn't move. He knew how deeply she'd come to care for him? Those were feelings she wasn't even admitting to herself.

"He feels it and this is the second time you've nearly killed him with your pain. Why do you think we told him to stay away from you? But you couldn't let it be. You drew him to you with your desire for him, asked him to protect you. How could he say no when he detects your grief, feels sorry for you?" Mei turned back around, her face filled with sorrow and anger. "You accuse me of things that aren't true. I feel close to Evan because he understands me and is there for me—as a friend. He's there for all of us and that innate understanding makes him family."

Josselyn glanced between Mei and Evan. Clearly Mei believed what she said, but could Josselyn? Evan did seem to know her, even when moody. When she looked in his eyes, she saw kindness and understanding.

"For some reason, you're more connected than others. You have a bad day and he..." Mei motioned to the medical booth. "He nearly dies."

"I didn't know," Josselyn whispered. The idea that she caused Evan's condition just by feeling gnawed at her insides. She would never wish harm on him.

"You didn't wish to know."

"Had I known..." Josselyn took a step for him. Loneliness threatened. She only just found Evan and now she had to let him go or kill him. What kind of choice was that? Why would fate rest so much loss on her? As the emotions hit her, Evan's lips parted in a painful moan. She gasped, pressing her hand over her chest, as if that simple act could force everything she felt deep inside. Josselyn buried the pain, the past, every emotion she could. As she did so, Evan blinked, his eyes opening. She whispered, "It is true."

"Rick is orbiting the fueling dock, but we must land soon. Evan should be all right for now, but for his sake please try not to feel anything." Mei moved to leave the room. "I'm going to tell the others he is awake."

"Josselyn?" Evan blinked, confusion passing over his face as he looked down his body being treated by the medical booth lasers. Most of them concentrated over his heart. "I can...explain."

His words were soft, gasping on each breath.

"Shh, there is no need." Josselyn made a move to touch him, only to glance down to the lasers and thought better of it. "Mei told me, but I should have known."

"I...should have...told..." Pale blue lined his lips, melting into the unbefitting pallor of his flesh. It was as if she'd drained the life out of him with her grief.

"I should have seen," Josselyn answered. "I think part of me knew by the way we understood each other, but I should have seen what I do to you. I meant you no harm, Evan. I do care for you and I thank you for everything that you've done for me. I wish there was a way I could repay you for your kindness."

"You're hiding..."

"Yes, I am," Josselyn laughed. "But it's for your own good that I keep my emotions from you. I don't think you're in any condition to handle them now, do you?"

"No." He shook his head.

"There he is." Rick strode into the room. "Sleeping on the job again."

Josselyn backed away. Rick gave her an easy smile. He was the only one. The others merely glanced her way as they gathered inside the small room. Josselyn found herself in the corner once more, pressed to the wall to stay out of the way.

"It says you're cured." Jarek pressed several buttons on the control panel. "Let's get him to his room. Sorry, Ev, but you're going to have to wait here while we dock."

Mei stood in the entryway, meeting Josselyn's passing gaze, only to draw it back and hold it. Josselyn nodded once in silent understanding. Mei stepped back, letting the others pass as they helped Evan walk from the room. Evan's head drooped forward and she wanted to join his side. Every instinct she had told her to follow, to sit by his side and care for him until he got better as a good protected woman should. But it was her nearness that had done this to him. The only way she could help him was to stay away. That is the understanding she had shared with Mei. To help Evan, she must leave him.

As the others left her alone, Josselyn crossed over to the medical booth. Now empty, the lasers had settled and shut off. Reaching inside, she touched the smooth panel where they'd focused on Evan's heart. The lights instantly turned on, flickering along her fingers. Warmth spread over the chilly digits, heating her like the licking flames of a fireplace. Just as suddenly as they started, the lasers stopped and the console beeped. Curious, Josselyn walked over to the unit. She recognized her name above several red flashing columns, but the star language writing was harder to translate.

She pressed the screen for more help. The console began to speak, the male voice distant and sterile as it lacked all emotion. "Passenger Josselyn Craven, medical status declining. Cellular deterioration of unknown origin. Incurable. Recommended treatments vary according to species culture, but are limited to heat treatment, pain management or ritual sacrifice. Comparing readings to the last known medical scan on file for this humanoid life form, death eminent in one to three weeks. Please send report case findings and preserved tissues samples to the Medical Alliance for Planetary Health for further study. Arrangements for burial or sacrifice should be immediately made."

As the unit spoke, Josselyn didn't move. She looked at her hands, the long, pale fingers even now shaking with cold. As she thought about it, there was a dull ache deep in her bones, just a hint, but there if she concentrated on finding it. Would it get worse? The unit recommended pain management.

"Or sacrifice," Josselyn whispered.

"Would you like to file a report to the Medical Alliance?" the unit asked.

Josselyn ignored it, continuing to herself, "If I

am to die, I might as well die with honor. *Ago pugna quod intereo per veneration.*"

"Would you like to engage override codes and delete entry?" the unit asked.

"Yes," Josselyn answered, leaning in to push a button to mark her choice.

"Entry deleted, please wait while all records are altered to original state."

"Live, fight and die with honor." Josselyn heard her father's voice saying the words with her. In her mind, she saw not the medical booth, but her front hall, her family, her brothers and mother. Suddenly, her path was clear. She didn't belong in this time. Fate knew it. Her dying body knew it. Too bad her heart and her head had been late catching up. She should have died a hundred years ago, shot in her father's study. Fate saved her. Fate brought her here and gave her just long enough to avenge the past.

"If you're still alive, Jack Stephans, I'm going to find you," she whispered. "And if you're dead, I'll dig up your grave and kill you a second time." Laughing softly, she glanced down at her chilled hand and felt no humor in her situation. "This time, we'll die together. We'll take our place in history where everything Craven belongs."

CHAPTER 17

"Evan asked that you stay onboard the ship," Jarek said. They stood in the cargo hold, the men rummaging through some of the crates for items to trade. Lucien was at her side, having found her in the commons waiting for the ship to dock. He'd brought her to Jarek, as the captain had requested. Standing before the giant cat-shifter man, a man who commanded everything around him with just a look, caused a shiver to overtake her that had nothing to do with cold and everything to do with apprehension. "He regrets that he is not able to take you, but promises to speak to you once he's well enough."

"Speaking to me is what causes him not to be well," Josselyn answered, seeing the truth of what Mei had told her in the captain's eyes. She didn't stand too close to Jarek, all too aware what a man like him would do if he thought someone betrayed himself or his crew. "I want to go with you to the fueling dock. The further away from him I am, the better chance he has at recovery."

Jarek seemed to struggle with loyalty to his friend and her logic before finally conceding to logic. He nodded once. "Very well. You may come."

"Thank you."

"You won't see him before you go, will you?" Jarek asked, slowly walking away from the others, toward a narrow pathway made by boxes in the cargo hold.

Josselyn absently followed him. She wondered at the question, only to assume it was her own guilt that made her read too much into it. "No. I think it is best if I leave him be. One slip of my thoughts, a little worry, and I could make his heart stop again. Don't ask that of me. I won't kill someone who saved me from prison."

"Stay by Rick once we land. He'll keep you safe when we split up. We have to restock the ship's supplies or we won't make it to another port."

"I understand." Josselyn nodded.

Jarek looked as if he'd say more.

"I will be fine," she assured him.

"Stay close to Rick," Jarek ordered. "Others you meet will not be trustworthy."

"I will be fine," Josselyn repeated, though his unnerving warnings were affecting her calm.

"Captain, what about this one? I think it'll fetch a nice price," Lucien called from behind some crates.

Jarek's attention diverted to the crew. He walked away to the far crates. "No, not that. It's illegal in this quadrant. We'll have to sell it in the Y."

Josselyn frowned as she was left alone. Slowly walking through the cargo hold, she noticed many of the containers had been painted black, and some not so well. Running her hand over the side of a particularly large one, she saw the old lettering imprinted into the newest layer of black paint. It had read, 'ESC'. Another read, 'HIA'. The telltale labels were only noticeable at the right angle, but they were there. Following the narrow path between boxes, she noticed other alien names with corporate logos. And then, a narrow, light brown trunk caught her attention. The color stuck out in the sea of blackness. She knew that trunk.

Running her hand over the familiar worn crest over the front, she pressed hard. The latches flipped open. Josselyn glanced around to see if the others heard her. They didn't and their debates on the other side of the hold continued as they tried to find what to barter and sell on the fueling docks.

Josselyn lifted the lid to the trunk. Inside, bright

colors flashed in the dim light. The Craven family jewels. These men had found her family's treasury.

"They're pirates," Josselyn said quietly, touching a ruby necklace she'd seen her mother wear to formal dinners. It all made sense—their lack of political alliance, the painted crates, some of the off comments she'd heard said amongst the crew. They were thieves and their mission to rescue her had merely been a raiding expedition prompted by the old holo-box they'd found.

Leaving the large ruby necklace, she picked up a strand of emeralds and slipped it over her neck. The loose shirt hid them from view. Again, she glanced over her shoulder. Josselyn unbraided her hair, quickly grabbing rings from the chest and slipping them over the strands as she re-plaited the locks in a more complicated design. So long as no one touched her hair, the jewels wouldn't be detected. It wasn't as if she stole them, they already belonged to her.

Indeed, it seemed fate had a hand in her present circumstances. It laid everything out for her. All she had to do was listen and follow where it led. And in the end, there would be only one regret. Never getting to say goodbye to Evan.

CHAPTER 18

ZIBI FUELING DOCKS

BARELY MORE THAN a hunk of floating space debris, the Zibi Fueling Docks hosted an unlikely number of alien species and reeked of sweat, spilt ship fuel and the faintest odor of cooking meat. They'd been recently renamed if the haphazardly marked out signs littering the platform were any indication. Even some of the workers had crossed out logos on their uniforms. Whatever it used to be called, there was no telling now.

Not associated with any planet, the docks rotated around a meteorite stuck in a dead moon's elliptical orbit. *The Conqueror* landed on the far end of the fueling platform, far from the main complex. According to the surly reptilian of a dockhand, they were lucky to even gain clearance for landing.

Mei stayed onboard nursing Evan and watching

her son. Josselyn didn't want to leave Evan without seeing for herself that he was all right, but there was no way to justify the risk. She would have to take the word of his friends.

As they walked single file along the length of the platform, steam hissed from rust spots in pipes that seemed to litter the interior walls. It made for sticky pockets of air they were forced to duck under. Alien ships ranging from rusted buckets of metal to luxury crafts lined the fueling pumps. Most were designs Josselyn had never seen.

Josselyn paused, stepping beside Rick as the other crewmen split into groups. Automatically, the men knew what they needed to do. Jarek and Lochlann stayed with the ship to supervise the fueling. Dev and Jackson carried a ship manifest to start bartering and selling. Lucien and Viktor went off to requisition supplies, including parts to fix the faulty ship communicators.

Furry bodies dwarfed pale slender figures, oblong blue faces bartered with small yellow ones, talons shook paws, paws clasped fingers, fingers avoided slimy knobbed hands, until no one looked normal nor out of place because everyone was the alien here. Josselyn stayed close to Rick's side, as they maneuvered through the large crowd. Metal creaked overhead, as if at any moment the ceiling would collapse and they'd all be sucked out into deep space. Alcoves fitted along the walls. Smoke curled from one, colorful billows of bright pink and yellow. The sound of music and laughter drifted along with it.

"Do you want me to take you back?" Rick whispered, his concern shining in such a way that only she could see it in him. "This is no place for a lady."

"I can't go back." Josselyn again turned her attention to the crowd, looking for someone, anyone she could approach. "Evan's sick."

"It's not your fault." Rick gave her a weak, unconvincing smile.

"Yes, it is."

"You didn't give him his powers." Rick pulled her arm slightly, as two hairy, fanged beasts sauntered by. "You didn't mean to hurt him."

"Intentional or not, I did hurt him."

"Know what you need?" Rick motioned inside the smoke-filled tavern. "A stout drink."

"But aren't we going for supplies?" Josselyn asked, searching the immediate area.

"My only task is to keep you entertained." Rick hooked her arm with his and pulled her into the darkened room. "And this place looks pretty entertaining."

CHAPTER 19

EACH BREATH HURT, not because of Evan's physical reaction to Josselyn's distress, but because with each breath he knew in his heart that she was going to leave him. He begged Jarek not to let her off the ship, but deep inside he saw the future. She was going to leave him.

Part of him wanted to fight the fog of sleep induced by the medical unit. It had injected him with something to make him rest and Mei ensured it would continue to do so by strapping the remote medical pack to his thigh. Another part of him argued to let fate take its course. He knew better than to predict an uncertain future, especially when the future involved his own. Meddling would only make things worse. Besides, he'd seen enough in his life to know there had to be something more—a higher power, a purpose, fate. He wasn't sure what to call it, but the force was there. Who was he to mess with its plan? The way his heart stopped was reason enough to let fate take its course, wasn't it?

But then, when did one fight fate?

Live, fight and die with honor.

"Mei," Evan croaked, pushing past his dreams. He wasn't sure if he spoke the words aloud, or if he merely screamed them in his head. His throat ached and they felt real. "Mei, stop her."

"Shh, Evan, easy," Mei answered, her words so far away it sounded as if she were trapped behind a wall.

"Stop her." Evan thrashed. *She's trying to leave me. I feel it. She's going. She's going. Jarek should not have let her leave the ship. You don't understand. If she leaves me, she'll only find death.*

MEI PLACED her hand over Evan's brow, stroking back his hair. His body didn't move except to occasionally shiver. He moaned, his parted lips quivering with deep breaths, as if he tried to tell her something. "She...find...death..." The words were incoherent babbling.

"Shh, Evan, easy," Mei whispered, her stomach tight with worry. She leaned over to the remote unit strapped on his thigh and pressed a button, hoping to ease him back to a restful sleep. "Easy. I'm right here."

CHAPTER 20

Josselyn watched a woman with five arms and a stump in place of a sixth dance with a furred beast whose hair wound in tight curls all over his body. The male's long arms and massive chest were covered with her many stroking fingers. Not wanting to stare, Josselyn diverted her attention to the side. Rick's head tilted back as he chugged a bright blue liquid, his eyes turned sharply toward the center square platform. A half-naked woman gyrated on stage, her gelatinous body wiggling in such a way that would've been impossible on a humanoid with flesh.

"I know our species aren't made for mating with that one, but I can't seem to look away."

Josselyn's eyes widened at Rick's low words.

"Did I say...?" Rick glanced at her. "Forgive me, my lady, I did not mean to speak aloud."

Josselyn lifted her glass of bright blue ooze and took a sip. The thick, stout liquor stuck in her mouth, nearly impossible to swallow as it seeped into her tongue like water into dry land.

Rick chuckled at her look. "An odd sensation, but you'll get used to it."

"Does not quench the thirst," Josselyn said.

"Not supposed to. It's supposed to get you drunk, fast." Rick grinned, even as he swallowed a big mouthful. "Told you we needed a stout drink. This is as stout as it comes."

Josselyn pushed her glass aside. Drunk was the last thing she wanted to be right now, but having Rick inebriated and distracted would work to her advantage. She again scanned the tavern. Long metal tables wound around the square platforms, each with a different alien dancer. But it wasn't the dancers who interested her, it was those watching from the sidelines—the travelers, the crews, but especially the captains.

"*Sacre*, he wasn't lying, was he?"

Josselyn glanced over her shoulder at the sound of a woman's coarse voice. Although definitely humanoid female, the tone had a deep drawl to it, a wryness that radiated in every bored syllable. Shortly cropped, curly brown hair danced around her chin as she moved. The slender tailoring of her outfit, tight drab brown pants and matching deep cut top, accented her tall figure.

The woman continued, "This place is a bucket of asteroid dust. I can't wait until we get to Rifflen."

Rifflen?

"Ship's about fueled, captain," one of the men with the woman answered. A large black horn protruded from the center of his blue forehead. It was cracked along the tip.

Josselyn's attention turned completely to watch as the woman passed. Green markings wound around her waist, imbedded in her skin, showing beneath the bottom hem of her shirt. She was young, surely too young to be leading the fearsome bunch who trailed behind her. A winged humanoid walked next to the cracked-horn alien. The blue-white of his feathered wings rested along his back-side, nearly touching the floor. Beyond the ridge over his naked chest, his front side looked to be as human as she. Behind them, a shorter male with webbed hands and green-yellow scales slithered over the floor, a long tail appendage replacing what would have been legs. Josselyn would have thought him a beast of burden if not for the stream of intelligent words coming out of his mouth as he spoke to the thin, ghostly pale man at his side. All of them were armed with gun-shaped weapons and dressed in a fashion similar to the woman—well, all but the tailed creature who was naked.

"That bastard general better give us double," the horned man said. "Uh, no offense, captain."

"None taken," the captain answered.

General? Rifflen? Josselyn tensed, her palms sweating as she watched the woman and her men take seats along the bar. Was this fate once again intervening, driving her toward her destiny, toward revenge? What else could it be? Here she was, looking for a way to get to Rifflen, to face a certain general, and she happened to overhear a conversation that would give her both the ride she needed to the very place she desired to go. It was a hard sign to ignore and unquestionably too big of a coincidence not to be preordained. She didn't have much time to live. Evan would die if she tried to spend those last days with him, as a large part of her wanted to do. She found the family jewels. This captain was going where she needed to go to see the very rank of officer she needed to find. Plus, it was quite possible her word, 'Sacre', was a bastardization of 'Sacrelue' a common curse for her people. Even if the general wasn't Jack, he would know where to find him or if he was alive. Perhaps he'd even be able to tell her what happened to her family, to her home, to her people.

The female captain reached down the front of

her shirt, grabbed a necklace, pulled the charm as she leaned forward and pressed the disc and her thumb against a small scanner. Rick had taken a similar thing out of his pocket to pay for their blue drinks.

"Can I borrow your coin? I wish to drink something else." Josselyn held out her hand to Rick and he supplied it for her easily. She walked to the long bar, close to where the female captain supplied the unit with her crew's drink orders. The woman didn't ask her companions as she typed in their drinks, signifying she knew them well.

Josselyn glanced back at Rick, but he wasn't paying attention to her. As she watched him, knowing what fate was pushing her to do, she ached with the knowledge that he would be her last connection to Evan. To leave Rick now would mean she would never go back to the ship. Inside, her heart beat fast and hard. But as much as the idea of leaving hurt, the knowledge that her staying onboard *The Conqueror* would kill Evan was worse.

Josselyn waited for them to say something else, so she could ease her way into their conversation. Soliciting rides wasn't exactly her area of expertise. Feeling eyes on her, she glanced to the side. The entire crew was looking at her, not moving.

"Need help deciding?" The captain pushed past the crew, shouldering her way in front of them. She placed her balled fists on her hips, her head tilted challengingly to the side. "Or you just have a problem with non-humans?"

Josselyn's eyes automatically darted to the tailed creature before she caught herself. His scales lost all green as he turned a bright shade of yellow and his body tensed, as if poised to strike. Josselyn shook her head.

"Then order your drink," the captain said, the tone darkening just like her green eyes.

Josselyn's hand shook and she was all too aware of the yellow thing staring at her. She lifted Rick's disc to press it against the scanner, only to draw back.

"Problems, moonbeam?" Rick asked from behind her.

Josselyn spun on her heels, the disc in her hand. "No. No problem." She followed his gaze to the captain. "They were helping me. It doesn't seem to work."

Rick chuckled. "Sorry, starshine, you need my scan. Forgot these things were picky. Damn security precautions, keeps an honest pickpocket from work." He took the disc, pressed it and his thumb to the pad. "Look up a whiskey for me, would you, dear heart?"

Josselyn nodded. Rick winked at the female captain, whistled low and went back to a different table to watch a new dancer. To the captain, Josselyn said, "I heard you say you were going to Rifflen?"

"What of it?" the horned man asked.

"How much to ride along?" Josselyn pretended to study the screen, scrolling through the drinks. Seeing whiskey, she pressed a button and continued to search, not really seeing the choices. Reading the star language took too much concentration.

"You and the man?" the captain asked.

"Only one of us." Josselyn watched the whiskey materialize beneath a clear panel on the bar top. When it was done, the glass of brown liquid was pushed up. Behind her, the music softened to a light twinkle. "I can pay in jewels?"

"Jewels?" the captain's voice rose in interest.

"Yes."

"I take it this is a fast departure?"

"Yes." Josselyn nodded.

"Well, we're heading there anyway. Half hour. Dock six. Lot five. Bring the jewels and we'll see if the ride is worth it." The captain tossed back her drink. "Come on, lads, let's leave this stink hole."

CHAPTER 21

Don't go, Josselyn...

Evan tried to pull away from the cool hand stroking his head, but no matter how hard he tried, it wouldn't leave. He didn't want that hand. He wanted Josselyn, but she was leaving. Each passing second visions of her swirled, deep and vivid within his mind's eye. He felt her presence, her fear and determination as if it were his own.

Her long fingers held a clear glass filled with dark brown liquor. It almost sloshed over as her hand shook with apprehension. She didn't want Rick to discover she was leaving, and part of her did. Josselyn wanted someone to stop her, but the others wouldn't. Evan was the only one who could reason her out of her decision to go and he was stuck in this dream, watching, helpless. She brought

Rick the drink, her face hazy in the smoke filled bar. Each passing second took her further away and there was nothing Evan could do to stop her.

Too late. Too late...

Josselyn, don't leave me.

GOOD JOURNEY AND A HAPPY LIFE, Evan Cormier.

Josselyn took a deep breath, glad that Evan wasn't anywhere near dock six. Slipping away from Rick had not been a great challenge. As the crowd in the tavern thickened with a new crop of travelers, new dancers graced the platforms. Rick, quickly falling deeper into his cups, drunkenly watched each and every one, his attention turning like the minutes of a ticking clock.

Josselyn kept her eyes averted as she navigated the crowd. With each fast step, she gained momentum until she practically jogged down the docking plank toward the specified lot. To her relief, the ship she found was not one of the piles of rust that parked along the planks, but nor was it a luxury ship. Much smaller than *The Conqueror*, it didn't appear made for long voyages. The sharp angles of its front nose turned upward at the end. Deep red stripes added an elongated effect to the shape, as they stood out from the almost too bright of the yellow ship's body.

"Got the jewels?"

Josselyn swallowed nervously at the tailed crewman. She nodded once. "Yes. But we must leave quickly before I am missed."

"Jewels," the tailed man demanded, his webbed hand extended.

"I'll give them to the captain once we're in flight," Josselyn countered, doing her best not to let the quivering in her body echo in the tone of her voice. She lifted her chin in defiance. Frightened as she was, she was still a lady and she could handle this situation.

"Then by all means, welcome aboard the *Racing Banana*." The tailed creature waved toward the yellow ship. "Fastest craft in these parts." If Josselyn wasn't mistaken, he smiled at her. "I'm Jo, your pilot for this trip." He slithered alongside the ship, reaching the back before shooting up the docking plank with amazing speed. His scales glimmered in the stark overhead lighting.

She followed him up, her gaze darting around the interior for the rest of the crew. Inside the ship, the winged man hovered over the floor, his large wings gently flapping. The man's hand extended and he somehow managed to get a bolt to tighten without touching it. Grease smudged his naked chest and arms.

"Gil, our mechanic," Jo said, pointing up.

"Josselyn," Josselyn said when Gil glanced down at her. He grunted and turned back to his work. "Pleasure to meet you, too." Gil grunted louder. She half expected Jo to make excuses for the rudeness. He didn't.

"Isaac," Jo pointed toward the cracked horn man as they passed him in the narrow hall. Josselyn couldn't meet the blue man's gaze, but that didn't stop him from watching her with piercing eyes. She felt them boring into her.

"Josselyn," Josselyn managed.

"Mm, I like them scared," Isaac said.

Josselyn tried to hurry past, but Jo's big body blocked the narrow passage.

"Leave her be," the female captain ordered.

Jo slithered out of the way. "And Captain Violette."

"Unless she doesn't have what she promised us," Violette continued, as if Jo hadn't spoken, "in which case I'll help you sacrifice her to the corg."

"I have it," Josselyn said quickly. "I'll give you half now, half when we arrive on Rifflen."

The captain held out her hand. Josselyn reached into her pocket and pulled out a sapphire pendant. The gold chain was gone, but the stone was big enough to tempt a crew like this on its own.

"What's to stop me from taking the rest from you?" Violette asked, giving a meaningful look at Josselyn's hip where the sapphire had been.

"You won't find them," Josselyn assured the captain.

"No?" Violette smirked, nodding once, a sharp commanding gesture.

Hands gripped her arms from behind. Josselyn gasped, struggling. "What?"

"Turn her," Violette ordered.

Isaac spun her around, only to grip her tight once more. He smelled sweet, almost sickeningly so as he kept her inches from his chest. The blue of his face terrified her, so cold looking even as it radiated heat. She struggled to be free, kicking at his legs. He didn't even grunt in pain, though she knew she landed some good blows.

"Don't waste your energy. He can't feel pain." Violette tugged violently at Josselyn's hair, snagging it as she slid jewels out of the plaited locks. When she'd gotten them all, she patted Josselyn on the head, brushed her now tangled locks aside and kissed her cheek. "Thanks for the payment."

"We had a deal." Josselyn tensed. How could she have misjudged the situation so much? What was she going to do now? Why would fate send her here only to be robbed by the crew of the *Racing Banana?*

"She's ice cold," Isaac said. "Her temperature has plummeted."

"Let her go," Violette ordered, her tone changing from mocking to something akin to concern. The captain touched Josselyn's shoulder, gently shoving her around to face her. Josselyn met Violette's steady green eyes. "You're not much for the game, are you?"

A shiver worked its way over Josselyn.

"Do not fret, love." Violette held up the sapphire pendant. "You can hold on to this if it makes you feel better." She forcibly pressed the jewel into Josselyn's numb hand. "It must be some man you're running away from."

"Yes, some man," Josselyn couldn't feel her arms, not like she should. Was it Isaac's grip on her that deadened her limbs? Did it stem the flow of her blood, keeping her from lifting her hands in combat? Josselyn looked down, seeing that Isaac didn't touch her. The medical booth had been right. She was dying. Thankfully, Evan was nowhere near her to feel her death. She would not kill him with her end.

Evan...

The word ached. The memory of his kiss haunted. She missed him terribly, so terribly her heart actually squeezed in her chest. Not even a day and she felt as if he'd been ripped away from her arms for much longer. How would she survive longer? A month? A year? A...

Josselyn took a deep breath, lifting her eyes from the sapphire pressed into her hand. There was no month or year for her. There would be no surviving. She swallowed down the pain, the memory of Evan. Today was not the day to cling to it. She had her duty to her family to concentrate on.

"How long?" Josselyn asked. "How long until we reach Rifflen?"

"Two days, three if the skies are against us," Violette answered. "Any particular sand dune you'd like us to drop you on?"

"The military base, if it is still there," Josselyn said. "Federation one."

"If it is there?" Violette chuckled. "Love, the military base is the only thing on Rifflen. There is nothing else."

"I wish to speak to the general," Josselyn continued. "Do you know him?"

"General Stephans?" Violette glanced to Isaac and Jo before nodding slowly. "Yes. We know him."

"Stephans," Josselyn whispered, her heartbeat quickening. Jack was alive. Fate knew what it was doing. "He is still..."

"Yes," Violette nodded. "I can arrange a meeting. Should I say who wishes to speak to him?"

"Jos... Just tell him my name is Evangeline Cormier." Josselyn didn't know why she chose that name, a name so close to Evan's heart, but it was the only one she could think of.

Jack was alive.

"You told us your name was Josselyn," Jo said.

"Josselyn Evangeline," Josselyn continued to lie. "No one knows me as Josselyn, not really."

"All right, then, Evangeline," Violette nodded, her face a blank, expressionless mask. "I say it's time we take off before your boyfriend comes looking. As much as I love a good fight, I like keeping my word and I have a shipload to deliver to Rifflen. If it's banged up, I'm out a quarter of a million space credits."

"Thank you for the ride." Josselyn knew the words were late in coming, but she said them nonetheless.

"Thank you for the jewels." Violette chuckled, waving at her crewmen. "Ready the ship for takeoff and show our guest to her quarters."

CHAPTER 22

Riding with Captain Violette and her crew of aliens did not compare to the luxury of *The Conqueror*. Josselyn thought it odd she had found *The Conqueror* lacking compared to her castle home for now she missed it terribly. Or more specifically, missed being near Evan.

Jarek and his crew did not give chase. There was no great race through the stars to get away. No one yelled her name or threatened the crew of the *Racing Banana* if they didn't turn around and give Lady Josselyn back.

Despite her conviction to push Evan from her mind, she thought of him constantly—of the way he looked at her, the way he touched her, the way he made her feel. He could make her happy with just one look, even when her world was falling to pieces at her feet.

Two days, though short by any measure, seemed to drag on like the long chore of scouring the castle hall by hand. Violette occasionally spoke to her, though her words were short, sometimes mocking, always secretive. Josselyn had to assume her nature was due to her station in life. Captaining a crew could not be an easy task. Whatever her mystery, Josselyn did not pry into it and understood she would never know the woman's history.

Her accommodations were a pallet on the floor of a cramped cargo hold. Dark green crates, piled from floor to ship's ceiling, surrounded her. Yellow numbers and letters marked their outsides, the only hint as to what was inside. Josselyn did not dwell on what lay hidden inside the crates. They didn't matter.

Jack lived, just as she had.

"No, not as I have," Josselyn whispered, her soft voice the only company in the dim room.

She pulled the thick covers, tucking them beneath her chin. The crew had given her many of them, noting whenever they happened to brush against her flesh how very cold she was. Curling into a ball, she burrowed into the soft depths. Her body did not generate its own heat and nothing seemed to banish the chill, which ached all the way to her deepest bones.

"Evan," she whispered, forcing Jack from her mind. She wanted to imagine something pretty, a life, a moment stretched on for eternity. Evan's smile. Evan's touch. Evan's kiss. She lived in that feeling, in the thought of what they could have been should life have given her a different lot. Married. In a castle surrounded by children. His sister. Her brothers. A family. A home. Peace. Happiness. Evan.

"I love you, Evan," she told the man inside her dreams, the husband he could have been, would never be. Her mouth moved within the make-believe memory. His eyes bore into hers. Castle walls surrounded them, glowing with the orange of fire-light. She was again a lady, dressed befitting the title, and he was her lord, the chocolate of his eyes deep-ened by the brown of his fine overtunic. "I wish I could stay with you inside this world. I wish fate cared for me as I care for you."

I love you, Evan. I should have told you before I left.

Sleep came to her softly as she imagined the blanket to be his arms, cuddling around her, keeping her safe.

I love you...

THE SKIES WERE NOT KIND, or so Violette commented, as they landed on Rifflen three and a half days after leaving the fueling dock. Turbulence rattled their landing, making the ship jump and lurch. By the time the mountainous white sand dunes came into view on the cockpit's viewing screen, nausea had taken permanent residence in Josselyn's throat.

Two thoughts kept her on her feet. The first of vengeance made her determined to see this through. Jack was on that planet or, in the very least, a descendent of Jack. Fate would not send her here if not to find him or his bloodline. The second thought was much sweeter for it was a memory of Evan and it gave her strength, even from a distance. She had no idea where in space he was, but she felt him and she clung to it.

"You're tinted blue," Violette said, eyeing Josselyn.

"Don't look at me." The blue-skinned Isaac chuckled. "I had nothing to do with it. She's not my type."

"If you can't walk straight, they'll scan you and put you in quarantine to make sure you're not a biological weapon sent to destroy the base," Violette continued. Then, arching a brow, she added, "You're not, are you? I'd hate to be the one to drop off the end to this decrepit, forgotten place."

Josselyn slowly shook her head in denial. On screen, the sand mountains shifted and moved, flowing like grainy water. Reminiscent of a tiny black fish jumping from an ocean's depths, a small platform raised from beneath the dunes. Sand blew over it, rippling and beautiful. The closer the ship flew, the bigger the platform became.

"Ah, there it is," Jo said, working frantically at the controls. Josselyn watched him from her chair. "I thought we'd have to make another pass. They must have reset their timer."

Josselyn glanced at Violette, not understanding.

"The platform only rises every half of an hour. The sand keeps transmissions from space nearly impossible, so ships dock and check in on the platform. It's the only way in or out," Violette said. "The base is under the sand."

"You can't land on the surface?" Josselyn studied the ever-changing planet.

"The ship would be swallowed up in less than an hour. Sometimes you can see old ships that were buried if you watch the surface, the sand pushes them out and sucks them back in. See, like there." Violette motioned to the screen to where a dark object appeared on the surface only to disappear. "A humanoid would be killed in seconds. If not buried alive, the sand would choke them. Keep watching long enough and you'll see bones."

"Then how was such a place built?" Josselyn shivered. She doubted she'd be leaving this place, not alive anyway.

"Alien contractors. Archorians can navigate the sand. They sift large polished stones from the surface. In return for building the base, they get Federation protection should anyone else want to sift the sands. Unfortunately for them, they got the worse end of the deal. No other species can survive on the surface. Their business is quite safe. They didn't need the Federation."

"Then, why?" Josselyn frowned. They neared the platform and Jo maneuvered the ship down the hollow center. Air blew up, making descent gradual as it kept the sands from entering.

As the column swallowed the ship and the ceiling closed over them, Violette answered, "General Stephans convinced them they needed the Federation. He's very persuasive, our general."

"Your general? Are you...?" Josselyn studied the crew. They didn't wear uniforms.

"It's an expression. We're not military. We're independently contracted." Violette laughed. "Think of us as shipment engineers. And you, my pretty cargo," the captain held out her hand, "owe us one shiny bauble."

Josselyn lifted the sapphire and handed it over to the captain.

"Now that we have all your valuables, you won't have a way out," Violette said.

"I'm not concerned," Josselyn answered.

The ship flew down, straight into the column. Bright light blinded the viewing screen, making them blink. Jo chuckled.

"Contact me when you're ready to go, we'll work something out." Violette's tone was low.

The bright light shone, tinting the world beneath Josselyn's eyelids a pale red. Cold crept into her chest from her limbs, freezing her heart and making icicles out of her hands and feet. It was all she could do to stay standing. She didn't answer Violette as she opened her eyes. There was no need. She would not be leaving Rifflen.

CHAPTER 23

"She all right?"

Josselyn looked up from the small table to the thin, pale woman who spoke. Skinnier than anyone she'd ever seen, the woman had a bendable, willowy grace to her movements.

"She's fine," Violette said, motioning the woman along. "Leave her."

The air was stale, but she seemed to be the only one struggling to breathe it. Though meant to mimic sunlight, the overhead lighting was a poor substitute to the real thing. Low ceilings, combined with the sand moving past the surrounding windows, made her think of being inside a tomb.

"Fitting," she whispered, watching the tiny grains shifting along the pane.

The smell of roasted meats and herbed vegetables drew her back to reality. She was in a restaurant on the Rifflen base with Violette's crew, waiting for her chance to talk to the general. Inside, she trembled. Outside, she did her best to appear calm. By the way people were looking at her, or pointedly not looking at her, told her she was doing a poor job of it.

Somewhere on this planet were the answers she sought, the reason fate woke her in this future world. Josselyn absently rubbed her fingers, trying to bring feeling and warmth back to them.

"Hey, Larry's back," Violette called, lifting her glass toward the wall of sand. A partially dressed skeleton had appeared, his arm appearing caught on a metal beam along the outside of the window by the sleeve of his tattered shirt. Sand moved through him like air, pressing him down so his bones moved like a stiff flag in a stout breeze.

"Larry!" those in the small restaurant cheered, lifting their cups, toasting the dead man.

"Ole Lar's been there since I was a little girl," Violette said.

"Mistress Evangeline?"

Josselyn glanced up at the gruff sound. A uniformed federation soldier stood at the table, dressed in the same matte black clothing she'd seen other soldiers in, his entire body stiff. The style was reminiscent of the federation uniform she remembered, only with straighter lines along the collar, which once had been rounded and smaller snaps in place of buttons.

"Are you Mistress Evangeline?" the soldier asked, staring at her like he didn't even see her.

"She's lookin' at you, isn't she?" Violette answered.

"Come with me," the soldier said.

"Go on," Violette told Josselyn. "It's why you're here."

"You have no idea," Josselyn said, pushing slowly up from the table. She felt as if her heart beat in her throat. Maybe it was her illness, her cold, numb limbs, or perhaps it was her time being so close to over, or was it Evan? Sweet, passionate Evan, whose face danced in her dreams and whose voice echoed in her heart. A warm spot in her icy death.

She regretted most of all not saying goodbye, not saying thank you, not saying she loved him.

Josselyn walked behind the soldier as he led her through the metal building. Outside the restaurant, the ceiling became higher as a long passageway led them toward the center. From what she could tell, the military base was shaped like a squashed sphere, tapering in height the closer one walked toward the outer edges. The center high point was where they entered. Doors lined the passage, each numbered in precise, militant numerical codes. Their closed entries hid any secrets.

"This way." The soldier turned, leading past the center docks, past the tall column that would expand out of the sands. Yellow lights flashed overhead, accompanying odd beeps. Below, workers aimed lasers at welded bolts, tediously reinforcing them one by one. They'd been doing the same thing when Josselyn's ship docked and she imagined they'd be at it for hours more.

"Why couldn't I have been born into that life?" Josselyn asked no one in particular. Suddenly, a mundane, repetitive existence sounded great. No duty or honor, only a laser and a row of bolts. Important and meaningless at the same time.

Clearly not hearing her full words, the soldier said over his shoulder, "The sand eats away at the welds so workers must go over them daily to make sure we don't get buried alive. They are some of the best marksmen on the base because they must do one row between each rising of the docking column."

Josselyn nodded absently.

"This way," the soldier ordered when her steps faltered.

This corridor was much wider, the metal walls covered with rich blue tapestries embroidered with a delicate white thread. Images of roadways and birds, orchards and villages passed her by as she walked. It only took a brief moment for her to realize it was home in the full of spring—everyone's favorite season.

The idea that Jack would dare to hang the image of her family home in his hallway irritated her. She held onto that anger, used it to keep standing even as her numb toes threatened to break off. The sound of the men working in the center of the base faded, replaced by music. She knew that sound. It was a festival, so long ago in this new time she lived in, yet not so far in her memories. Home. Family. All that was taken away reverberated in that song. And he who had taken it away was behind that door listening to it. Fate sent her here to avenge her family. She knew she would see Jack again, never really had questioned he would be alive and here. Foolishly, she had not thought to have brought a weapon. But if fate had orchestrated all this, surely fate would not let her fail.

The thick oak door seemed out of place in the metal construct. Its carved patterns spoke of crafts- manship and time. The soldier touched the metal latch, confidently opening the door like a servant. The music became much louder. He bowed slightly, not entering. "The general is expecting you, mistress."

Walking into the general's quarters was like

walking into her father's hall. A barren fireplace graced one wall, surrounded by emblems and even a banner with the Craven crest. The music lowered as her eyes traveled over the decorated wall toward a red cushioned chair near the corner. Though part of her knew not to expect a youthful Jack, the old man surprised her. Despite the shortly cropped grey hair and the distinguished wrinkles lining his lips and eyes, she knew his gaze. Steel green stared at her, steadily searching her face as if she were a dream. He wore white, like the last time she saw him, only this time it wasn't shiny but a dull cotton-like blend. The long tunic hung to his knees, slit along the sides to show loose matching pants. A thick brown stripe ran along the side of his legs and arms.

"Josselyn," he whispered, the sound faint, as if frightened he'd scare her away. His hand lifted, the fingers extended. "You've come. I almost gave up hope that you would. When the alarms on the prison complex were activated and then the old castle, I had to see for myself. The imager we put on the weather satellites turned on and we saw them carrying you from the grounds. The image was grainy and blurred, but I mean, it had to be you. Everyone else we'd moved, but you wouldn't fit through the door and down the narrow stairwell. I was told you'd been crushed like everyone else, but then there you were, like you'd been waiting all these years to come back to life. I'd hoped, dreamt of you waking up to face me, but I never had the nerve to see your crushed stone face for myself and the Federation banned anyone from going back. That's why they had the sensors—"

"Jack." Her tone wasn't as soft or wistful as his. She turned, her feet shuffling as she faced him fully. They were alone in the room, but she didn't trust him and his ready words, so easily given, gave her reason to pause. The speech sounded practiced, as if he'd thought of what he would say to her. She endeavored to see past the wrinkles along his eyes, the smooth skin of his cheeks that pulled too tightly and stretched his once youthful lips.

"Ah, I rush too fast to tell you everything." Jack nodded. He touched his cheek briefly. "How strange I must look to you with my age."

"You look like a traitor." She took a step for him, scanning the immediate area for weaponry. Why hadn't she grabbed a laser in the center dock? One of those bolt sealers would have done the trick.

"History remembers me as a humanitarian." His light laugh irritated her.

"History is only a record of those who have no idea. We know the truth, don't we, Jack? We know what you did." A shiver worked over her spine and a lock of her own hair tickled the side of her neck.

She stretched her cold fingers, each agonizingly stiff movement a painful reminder of her impending demise. The ache got worse, spreading up her wrists and forearms. Soon it would creep up her shoulders and neck. How soon until it reached her heart and lungs? Her body begged her to curl into a ball on the floor, to close her eyes to this nightmare and never wake up.

Soon. Very soon.

"I've changed since that day." Jack stood. If she'd expected a feeble, shaking shell of what he once was, she would've been mistaken. "I am not that young, foolish man."

"I'll tell you what you will never be." She managed to arch a brow. "Lord Craven."

"Hm," Jack gave a small smile, as if enjoying his own joke.

"No matter how many things you put my family crest on."

He carried himself well and she couldn't help but marvel at the medical advances that had made his life so long and healthy. In many ways, seeing him thus, having lived full and long was beyond unfair. "You don't look well, Josselyn. Please, have a seat. It can't be easy standing. I see how pale your hands are and I imagine your feet and legs are about the same."

"I want nothing from you, not even a chair."

"Then you aren't the girl I remember. The Lady Josselyn I knew would want the reason why I did what I did. She'd want to know what the last century had brought, how her home became a block of ice."

Josselyn tried not to stare at him, but it was hard to look away from the steel green of his eyes. Glancing down, the ring on his finger caught her attention. Though not her father's ring, the symbol was an exact replica. Rage boiled inside her. "You dare to wear my family's crest? You dare to hang it on your wall like it was your own?"

"Sit, Josselyn." Jack motioned toward the chair he'd abandoned. "You appear to be in the last stages of the illness. I know you cannot be comfortable swaying about like you are."

Josselyn didn't move, not surprised by his words. It figured he'd know what was wrong with her, was somehow responsible. She didn't need his concern or his charity. She considered questioning him on her illness, but held back, not wanting him to know she was weak. "You took everything from me."

"The Federation's course of action was unfortunate, but they did what they felt they must." This time his words weren't as rushed. "Rebellions had erupted on some of the other moons and they feared others would soon follow. The decision was made to strike first to minimize losses." Jack strolled to the desk and poured himself a drink from a crystal decanter. Josselyn turned slowly, keeping her gaze on him. The Craven crest was etched into the side of the decanter. "I never meant for you to get hurt. By the time I discovered the massacre, it was too late to stop it. Your family was already gone." Lifting the glass to his lips, he paused. "I'd offer you some, but it'll only make your condition worse." He gave a short, humorless laugh. "Not that you'd take anything I had to offer you. I suppose we both know why you're really here."

"I saw you, Jack. You were a part of the massacre and we only fought to defend our homes from the tyrannical oppression of the Federation." Josselyn moved toward the desk. She hated to be closer to him, but she needed to support her weight with something and the desk was the most logical place to search for weapons. Now that she was here, she realized how poorly she'd thought about her revenge. Maybe the numbness in her limbs had spread to her mind.

"I didn't want to be, but once it was started, once your father knew I'd helped the Federation, I couldn't change sides. He would not have forgiven me. He never treated me like a son. A son he could have forgiven for foolish youth, but me? I was no more than a Craven responsibility. There was no real choice. I had to choose and I chose preservation. I hoped your father and brothers would see the light, that they would see in the favor of progression, of advancing the moon alliances." Jack sipped his liquor, a slow movement, as if he'd waited years to say these words and was taking his time to make sure they were exactly as he'd practiced. "The planet of Florencia understood that. The old treaties gave them the right to decide."

"We govern ourselves. That is true freedom. The old treaties were ancient, when our ancestors first came to the planet. It was only by some scholarly inquiry that the old law was even found." Josselyn gripped the desk, barely feeling more than pressure beneath her palms. Why was she debating moon law and treaties? None of those really mattered anymore. *"Ago pugna quod intereo per veneration'."*

"Honor? War was coming, but you all didn't want to see it. The Federation was too big and swords and stones were no match for the weapons of modern age. Better the Federation than one of the alien species they wanted to protect us from. You always thought so small. Do you think the leaders on the planet of Florencia were our biggest threat?"

"We were handling ourselves and there was no alien threat. Those were propagandist lies to make us concede."

"We were part of a dying age, as historic as the time you tried to recreate. The past cannot be redone, no matter how hard you try to remake it. What happened would happen. The only change we could have effected was which side we came out on—victors or the conquered. I chose to be a victor and so I lived."

A sharp pain seized her legs and she let out a small cry as her knees tried to buckle beneath her. Hard knots contorted her calf muscles, making it near impossible to stand without the help of her hands.

"I'm sorry it hurts so badly. Would you like something to ease the pain?"

She glared at him. Her fists balling. She knew it was useless, and still she swung her arm. To her surprise, she caught him off guard, slugging him across the jaw. Jack's head snapped back. She swung again, but this time he was ready, catching her fist in his. With one deft maneuver, he had her back pinned to his chest.

"You are in no condition to fight," he said.

"I will die fighting," she answered.

Jack let her go. Josselyn fell against the desk, breathing hard.

"We didn't know the complications that would arise from the reversal process when we imprisoned you. Honestly, we thought we were doing the humane thing. By imprisoning you, we could later bring you back to reason with, one by one. Not everyone had to die." Jack dared to touch her cheek. "It was never my intention for you to be held captive so long, but a full war broke out on the other moons. The rebels were eventually squashed, though the weather systems were hit before the end. A scientist said their blast points would make for easy repairs to put the moons to rights. All it did was make the weather unpredictable as the satellites limped on for years. Incidentally, the man wrong about that little laser blast was also the one who invented the 'safe and reversible' prison holding process you're now dying of. His addiction went undetected a little too long. It seemed the only invention he got right was a synthetic pleasure drug undetectable by Federation and MAPH protocols."

"How sweet it must be for you to see me tortured thus," she whispered.

"I loved you, Josselyn," Jack said. "It seems silly to me now, me an old man and you..." He reached as if to touch her cheek, his hand hovering when she flinched. "You are almost exactly as I remembered you. How many times I've imagined this conversation."

"I—"

"No, don't speak." Jack withdrew his wrinkled hand, letting it fall to the desk to mimic her grip on the thick oak. Red marred his jaw. "I know all the questions you must have. I've thought of them and more. I always hoped one day you'd come. I hoped fate would make it so."

Josselyn didn't move. It was easier not too. Jack knew fate had a hand in this moment. Is that why he wasn't surprised by her arrival?

"The Federation made their prison camps on the dead moons they had created, only to abandon them when a new star system showed itself and a new war emerged. All their grand plans died with the last of our weather nearly eighty years ago. None of the things we hoped to accomplish, all the protection they were to have given us, was gone. I fought for years to get permission to free the prisoners, to free you, to get funding on a cure for the ice sickness. Unfortunately, those who released you didn't know. No one knows of the misfortunes that befell the prisoners or our world. Those who freed you doomed you."

A glint of metal caught Josselyn's gaze. Long and thin, she wasn't sure what it was, but the blade seemed sharp and her family's crest was engraved on the silver handle. Anger boiled, giving her a sudden surge of strength. How dare he say things like "our world"? How dare he speak of her family and use her crest? She was the last Craven. This was her crest. Not his. The tragedy he spoke of with such a regretful voice was her tragedy. Not his.

"Are you sure I can't get you something for the pain?" Jack said softly. "I think you should take something."

Josselyn made a weak noise, a cross between a cry of outrage and a sob of heartbreak. Her nose burned with all the tears she had yet to shed and never would. Moisture froze in her eyes, almost as cold as her flesh. Without thought, she gripped the slender hilt and swung. There was a moment of victory as the blade met flesh and it was much harder than she thought it would be to push it in. But her hand was already moving and she couldn't stop it.

A sound of surprise echoed and she looked at Jack's face. His lips were set in a grim line, as if he had expected and anticipated her blow. The sound had come from her own lips. She had done it. She stabbed Jack.

Revenge.

Death.

"Jack?" Warmth covered the cold of her fingers and she looked down to see blood trailing from the wound. The blade protruded from his chest, just below where his heart would beat. This moment didn't feel like she thought it should.

"Ah," Jack said at last, a halted sound as he let

go of the breath he held. He gave her a slight smile. "I knew you would be the end of me. I knew." Blood trickled over the side of his mouth, running crimson down his chin. "It is fitting that we finish this together."

She felt a sting in her arm. Jack held a needle against her, injecting light green liquid into her arm. Josselyn jerked away, but it was too late. The action caused her knees to buckle and she fell against the desk, sliding helplessly to the floor. The needle stuck out of her arm. Jack's glass of liquor fell over, rolling over her head and barely missing her shoulder as it tumbled to the ground.

Jack wobbled on his feet as he walked toward his chair, collapsing into it. The blade still stuck from his ribs and he made no move to take it out. "Just as things should happen."

Fire burned up her arm and she wanted to scream, but she didn't have enough energy left.

"By the time we found a cure and I had the permission necessary to give the command to have your statue transported to the laboratory, the bases were being abandoned because of the snow storms plus I learned that the warden had been ordered to destroy the statues. Apparently, watching over the Federation's mistake became too much of a hassle, especially with the storms. By that time no one knew whom they guarded. They believed the prisoners to be virus carriers whose death was an act of mercy. Then they were forgotten by everyone, erased by other events and people like they were never there."

Josselyn glanced at her burning arm, to the old-fashioned syringe sticking from it. The limb wouldn't move, no matter how hard she tried to make it work—not even a finger tremor. She flicked her other hand up at the vial, pushing it from her arm. But it was too late. Whatever he'd given her, it was inside her body.

Jack coughed. "Don't you worry about that. It'll take all your pain away."

"Only way you could be assured I'd stay and listen to you?" Josselyn's raw throat stung, the glands under her jaw swollen and tender.

"It's strange, but there is so much I should tell you and I find now, looking at you, I don't want to admit to it. But I need you to hear the full story."

"Could you hurry up and die first?" She took a deep breath. "That is what we're doing here, isn't it?"

"Only three days after all the prisoners were crushed and abandoned a cure for what ails you was discovered by scientists, but it was too late, they had killed them all. So out of all the planets, two were freed. Two who were lucky enough to be left in the laboratory far away from the moons. A simple, every day, un-political man and a woman who would later become my wife."

"Wife?" Josselyn gave a weak, derisive laugh. "Of course you married. Who was she? Some meek mannered simpleton who didn't know what you'd done?"

"Yes," he answered to her surprise. "Though simpleton is a little harsh. Your mother might not have been intelligent when it came to politics and social issues, but she was a kind-hearted woman."

"You think—" Josselyn stiffened. "My mother? She's alive?"

"Sadly, no. I lost my wife years ago."

"Your wife?" Josselyn couldn't breathe. She gasped for air. The pain seizing hold of her heart had nothing to do with her illness. No. He lied. Her mother would never... No. Not with Jack. No. A tear streamed down her cheek.

"By the time she was released, I was older than her in years. I understood her and could protect her. She was not made for a world beyond the Florencian moons. As far as I knew, she was the last of the Cravens and I made it my life to take care of her."

"And you would do anything to claim my father's title, wouldn't you?"

"I wanted to marry you, Josselyn. That would not have given me your father's title. I wanted to be a part of your family. Is that so wrong?" He grunted, his sudden, irritated movement causing a shudder of obvious pain to roll over him.

"I never loved you, Jack."

"I know. I do. But you never tried to either. If it helps you to forgive her, your mother was never the same after discovering the loss of her family. Of course I spared her the details, tried to make her happy, to give her a semblance of her life back, but I think the pain of losing all of you finally killed her."

"I have no problem forgiving my mother. She was too pure to understand you and your ways. Deception was not in her nature and she did not look for it in others. But you, Jack. You, I will never forgive. I already know without you telling me that she didn't know your part in it. In fact, she probably was convinced that you were the hero she always said you could be." Unsure how, she leaned forward, crawling across the floor, pulling her weight forward with one arm as the other dragged along the rug. Her eyes locked on Jack's steeled ones. His pale features set in a stoic expression.

"I've only one last thing to tell you."

"Speed you to a quick end?"

"No." Jack shook his head. His hand wrapped around the hilt of the blade and she wondered if he would try to defend himself. "That, as your replacement father, I have your inheritance safely locked away." His fingers lifted from the blade, reaching higher into his tunic. He pulled out a small disc and motioned toward her. It slipped from his fingers and landed on his lap. "For you and—"

"Josselyn!"

She turned her attention toward the door in shock. "Evan?"

"There is your ride. Earlier than I would have liked." Jack grunted, as he again grabbed the hilt poking from his chest. "My death will not be a sin you live with."

Josselyn stared at the door as the thick wood crashed open, hitting upon the metal wall with a hard, resounding clank. Evan was there? How was that possible? Had he followed her? Did he come for her? Her heart soared until she felt the burning sensation spreading toward her chest. If she died and Evan was near, would he be free or would she kill him? The support of her good arm crumbled and she collapsed on the floor. Still, her eyes watched through a mess of hair as Evan came fully inside the room.

"Evan, no!" She tried to scream, but the words were a hollow whisper. "Don't come in here. This is not where you should be."

CHAPTER 24

"Josselyn," Evan yelled, half commanding, half questioning. All the worry he felt since waking up to learn she'd slipped past Rick cumulated into this one moment. It didn't help that they planned to let her escape, left her family jewels where she could find them, found a reputable captain going to the Rifflen base and made arrangements for her safe, yet unaware, passage. Jarek had known she would try to find the general for he understood the nature of vengeance. Nor did it help that Mei had somehow slipped one of the ESC homing beacons into the material of Josselyn's shirt. The beacon would track her and assure she got where she was going.

Aside from when Mei forced him to sleep with a shot from the hand-held medic, Evan had stayed awake, staring at the viewing screen in the cockpit, hoping for just a glimpse of the ship they followed. Rick stayed behind, flying right on the edge of all standard radar detection range so they could not be seen.

Evan understood why the others had done it. They couldn't take her with them because of his health. Her nearness was literally killing him. None of the others were sure if she would trust them, so they did what they had to do. Their only choice was to drive her away and they did, like a perfectly orchestrated plan, understanding she would do the only thing she could in her situation—find revenge.

Now he saw her, pale and weak on the floor, beneath an older version of the general from the hologram. Jack stood above her, a bloody slim dagger in his hand, poised as if he would collapse upon her with the blade. Evan didn't think, just acted as he lifted the laser. It didn't matter that he was on a federation base, that he was a highly decorated general, that to fire this shot would mean his death. He pulled the trigger, the quick blast shooting from the end and finding its mark right in the general's heart. To Evan's surprise, he felt the briefest sense of relief come from the man as the general gave him the smallest of smiles before the life faded from his gaze. Almost instantly, an alarm sounded in a series of two short beeps and one long, repeating.

As the general's body slid to the floor, Evan rushed forward, trying to reach Josselyn before she was crushed by the dead man's weight. Jack fell across her legs and she cried out.

"Josselyn, I'm here," Evan said, pulling her by her arms. She didn't fight him, only moaned. He felt her numbness and it scared him. Running his hands over her body, he searched her for wounds, for the source of the bloody dagger. He found it, not with his hands, but with his eyes. The red stain spread over the general's chest. The blood was his. "I've got you, starshine. It's over. You're safe now."

"Ev," the whisper was so soft it could have been a gasp. With the loud alarm it was too hard to tell.

"Not yet," he demanded. "You cannot die yet. We should have more time. I saw us having more time. I knew this would—"

"Back away! That is the general's heart alarm. He's dead." A woman shouted. "You have your orders. As his heir, I'm in charge now until the federation sends his replacement. This base operates on the old codes and I invoke my rights."

Evan maneuvered his arm under Josselyn's legs, ready to lift her. A woman walked in, hard green eyes rolling over the whole scene. She wore tight black pants and shirt. The long sleeves were cross-laced together from shoulder to wrist with white ties. Her shutter of grief was real and controlled and mixed with disgust and pity. The composed expression didn't change. Evan understood immediately that Jack was her father.

"Just as he said it would be," the woman stated. "I didn't want to believe him, but he has been waiting for her my whole life. He told me she would come to end him, his ghost lady."

"You don't understand what is happening here," Evan said to the woman. "You can't."

"I understand that a very young girl swore a blood oath to her father." The woman tugged at her tight sleeve, lifting it to show a long scar on her forearm. "I understand that today that oath has been fulfilled. But, mostly, I understand that once Josselyn is safely off this base and the affairs of my father are wrapped up neatly and a new general is in place, my obligation is over. I will come for her. I will come to avenge my father, for unlike him I do not forgive her. When she wakes, tell her Captain Violette sends her regards."

"There is no need. She's dying. Your father killed her years ago when he imprisoned her into stone." Evan lifted her up. Josselyn's arm flopped to the side. "I recommend you find a better use of your energy. Revenge will only eat away your soul."

"There is a chance she will survive." Violette crossed the room, going toward her father. She lifted a needle off the floor. "He gave her the antidote. He might have killed her, but he also saved her." Then, pulling a disc key from beside her father's hand, she tossed it at Evan. He caught it, barely, as Josselyn almost fell from his arms. "That is for her. The safe is on Quazer in the Glamour District. I'm revoking your ship's permission to stay on the grounds because they refuse our standard inspection. Your shipmates have been unharmed and await you on the ship. I recommend you take her and go."

"Thank you," Evan said, feeling foolish. He just shot the woman's father and she was letting them go. There seemed to be a deep story there, but he wasn't sure he wanted to hear it. His emotions were full from Josselyn, he couldn't handle Violette's.

"Get out of here." Her voice rasped, catching slightly.

Evan didn't need to be told again. He carried Josselyn from the room. Pulling her tight, he moved past the guards waiting down the hall. They eyed him, their jaws set, as if memorizing his face. Behind him, he felt Violette's anger slip. He imagined her to be over her father's body, slamming her fists into the man's dead chest, cursing Josselyn and the oath the general had made her take.

Evan blocked Violette from him, cutting her off. It wasn't hard with the numbness of Josselyn filling his veins. Each step was labored and he felt her death eating at him. Would he ever be able to be near her without feeling so much? When she was gone, he'd thought of her, wanted her to the point his body stung and his senses ached. It was a bitter-sweet torment. He felt like he was dying without her and knew he would die with her.

Unsure how he managed, he found himself at the end of the corridor in the center docks, gripping Josselyn tight in his trembling arms. *The Conqueror* was there, waiting with engines on. Guards eyed him as he passed. No one moved, but their hostility snapped in the air. The alarm stopped blaring and was replaced by the hum of the ship.

Dev waited at the end of the docking plank with Jackson, his arms crossed in a threateningly composed position as his black eyes stared down the surrounding guards. It was as if he dared them to try and breach the ship. Evan knew they wouldn't. Violette had given her orders that they remain unharmed.

"Jackson," Evan called, stumbling. The man rushed down the plank, trying to take Josselyn from his arms. Reluctant to let her go, but unable to force strength to his weakening limbs, he released her. Feeling a pull behind him, he glanced over his shoulder. Violette stood, arms crossed, watching Josselyn disappear inside the ship with Jackson.

"Walk straight," Dev whispered gruffly, grabbing Evan's arm and practically dragging him up the plank. "We don't want to be stuck here waiting for the next chance at takeoff."

Overhead another alarm sounded, punctuated by the sound of metal clanking metal. The center column began to lift. Dev let go of him as they neared the top of the plank. Instantly it lifted, closing behind them. And, as he glanced through the narrowing view of where the plank lifted to meet the side of the ship, he saw Violette still stared. Her eyes met his and she nodded once before turning her back on them. Evan saw the challenge, the warning, but there was nothing he could do. His worry was for Josselyn. She was all that mattered.

CHAPTER 25

THE HEAT BURNED, setting her veins on fire and boiling her blood until it seemed to bubble out of her flesh in a sweat-soaking nightmare of pain. A weak moan filled her ears, but the voice was strange, not hers. Or maybe it was. It became too hard to tell.

Why wasn't she dead? Or was this death? Did her final act of vengeance earn her a spot in eternal hellfire? Should she have asked for forgiveness?

Where was her family? She expected to see her family—her father and brothers, standing and waiting at the end of some black hole at a bright light in the stars. Their faces smiling, the blood she'd last seen on them all gone. But there was no family.

Then she thought of her mother, of what Jack said and the burning became worse, focusing on her heart. Her mother married Jack. The elder Lady Craven never knew the truth and she died married to Jack. Had she been happy? A prisoner? Insane? If she'd gone crazy, that would make sense. For Josselyn couldn't believe that her mother could love Jack as she'd loved Lord Craven.

She might be dead, but this wasn't heaven. There were no happy families, no peace. The fire turned her thoughts back to her body. This had to be hell. Nothing but fiery pain and tormenting thoughts of things she could not change as she floated in darkness.

EVAN WASN'T sure how long he was locked in Josselyn's dark dreams, but as he clawed his way out of them, he felt as if he understood more of her than he had just feeling inside her emotions. Images came to him, her images, of her past, of her family. At first, they were images of bloody bodies in her home, of gasping dying breaths, of young Jack in shiny white.

But as the pain within them lessened, so did the darkness of her dreams. Dead bodies turned to live ones, of first frowns and serious conversations about the government on the planet of Florencia trying to take over the individual moons, about money, land

and power. Conversations with her father and brothers about shiny objects given to get the masses to spy on their leaders, of moles within the Craven house, of swayed votes and of the secret group Josselyn and her family helped form to fight back. Then the planet of Florencia joined the Federation and chaos broke loose. The domineering govern-ment met with resistance and Evan could guess the rest from what he knew of her, Jack and the nature of the Federation itself.

The Federation would not wait patiently for Florencia to comply. They would give an impossible timeframe, get angry when that timeframe wasn't met and then they'd kill the head of the Florencia government, and claim the lands under a hidden treaty clause. From there, the moons would have been attacked using the colony spies against them. Prisoners were taken, this time put into stone. They destroyed much, blowing up the weather satellites, killing the territories they thought to want. The moons died, were abandoned and the Federation, without blinking, would have gone on to their next war with only a greater number of foot soldiers recruited from the destroyed masses to show for their victory. Time had passed, new commanders would have risen in the Federation's ranks and the moons and prisoners would have been forgotten.

The pieces of her story fit together neatly in his

mind, not that it affected the way he was feeling. He cared for her and worried that what he felt was empathy, not love. But did it matter where love came from? If he felt it and it felt real, if he dreamt her dreams, wanted nothing more than to hold her, was willing to risk death just to be with her, wasn't that love? He didn't feel like this with Samantha. Sam was like his sister, his love for her platonic. Josselyn was...

"Different," Evan whispered, blinking in the dim light of his quarters invading his sight. He took a breath, barely able to believe that the pain had released its hold. All the memories stayed and he felt closer to Josselyn than he'd ever felt to anyone. For an empathic soul, that said something.

"Josselyn?" Again his voice was a hoarse whisper. Worried that he felt no one with him in the room, he reached to his side, to where he'd made the others promise to leave her. They probably just took her to the medical unit for testing.

Evan's hand hit against cool, unmoving flesh. His heart skipped and he sprang into action. Josselyn's pale face was turned toward him, buried in a sea of her long, brown hair. Her expression was so serene in its beauty and yet it was the most horrific image he'd ever seen. He grabbed her wrist, running his thumb to her pulse, knowing before he felt for life that there would be no responding thump of her heartbeat.

Zhang An's curse. The full reality of it came over him.

'Together you travel and together you'll remain. Tied and joined like the five elements of our people. The road to happiness is very rocky for all of you… But fate is not clear. If you do not recognize it, you will lose it and be forever alone.'

Had he resisted his fate too long? Is this why he no longer felt her? She was dead?

"Joss?" He managed, choking over his panic. "No, Josselyn."

CHAPTER 26

"IT'S OVER, SWEET DAUGHTER."

Josselyn gasped, opening her eyes. The darkness and pain eased and her body felt light as if the very breeze drifting through the castle would pass through her. Whispering, she looked at the front hall of her castle home. The warm spring air surrounded her, smelling of wildflowers and berries. "I am home?"

"Yes, we are all home."

Josselyn blinked, glancing around at the familiar sound of the late Lady Craven's soft, melodic voice. The noblewoman looked exactly as Josselyn remembered her, not some older worn version who would have married Jack.

"Mother? What happened? How did I get here?" She was too scared to move. "Is this real?"

"You came here the same as us," Lady Craven answered, moving slightly so Josselyn could see her father standing behind her, and her brothers standing further still behind the noble couple. Her siblings approached, their movements as leisured as limbs swaying on the wind. All were there, smiling and perfect—Jonathan, Peter, Ralphe and Rainier. "We found each other in the afterlife, as we were meant to."

Around them, the hall seemed to blur like the very edge of a dream, hazy yet there. Her mother gently touched her cheek. "It is there, my daughter, as real as it ever was. This is our reward for leading an honorable life. Our eternal peace."

Josselyn shivered, instantly covering the hand with her own. Her mother's scent, honey with just a hint of lavender, wafted through her. Lady Craven's skin was as soft as she remembered, smooth and perfect.

Jonathan stood, tall and proud, his face set in the serious way she loved. His short brown hair was cropped close to his head. Peter, their scholar, with his mussed up locks and crooked smile nodded in her direction. Ralphe was more a lover than a fighter, though in life he'd been proficient in both pastimes, grinned and winked audaciously. And finally, Rainier stood hands on hips, young and pleasant with a proud face and eyes full of mischief.

"The things Jack said about you," Josselyn told her mother, not able to believe the general's words now that she saw her parents together.

"I was not the same in life after the death of all of you. I was lost and he was the only thing from the world I knew. He was not a bad man in the end, but he had to pay for what he'd done in order for us to find peace, together as a family. No amount of humanitarian work can erase a sin as great as he'd committed. In the end, we pay for our choices. You have avenged us, Josselyn. Now we can be together. It is over."

Josselyn's smile faded.

"What is it?"

How could she say Evan's name now, in the presence of her family? Her heart ached to go back to him, to fight for life, but perhaps it was too late for that. Besides, every time she went near him, she inevitably almost killed him.

"Nothing," Josselyn lied. "I just can't believe that you all are here and well."

Rainier laughed. "We're dead. Does that count as being well?"

Ralphe stepped forward, his movements were unhampered in the brilliant paradise surrounding them. They were home, all of them. She looked over her brothers, all smiling and youthful, so happy it made her heart flutter with relief.

Every instinct inside her bade her to tease them, to forget all but the feeling of lightness and home. Well, every instinct but one—her desire to see Evan again, to say thank you, to say she loved him for however brief their time was, to say goodbye and to say she wished it wasn't the last time they'd meet.

"Not all of us," her father said, his hand lifting.

They knew about Evan? Josselyn gasped. "Father?"

"There is one more we shall welcome as our own." Lord Craven slipped his arm around his wife's slender waist. "Another child I will claim as my own when the time comes."

Lady Craven gazed at her husband, smiling sweetly and with graciousness. "I did not deserve you in life and I do even less in death."

"Right you are, my angel," her father chuckled. "But I do love you for lowering your standard and staying with me anyway."

Lady Craven giggled and Josselyn knew both parents understood that was not what her mother had meant by her words.

"He will come here, then? If I wait? If I am patient? He will come to join us?" Josselyn asked.

"She," her mother said.

"She?" Josselyn shook her head in confusion.

"A sister," her father answered, hugging his wife tighter.

"You and Jack? A daughter?" Josselyn whispered, understanding. Then Evan would not someday come.

"She is a good soul, troubled but one who will find her way to us eventually after she's lived her life. I regret that I was not the mother to her that I was to you, but she is still our family." Lady Craven dropped her hand.

"I will welcome her as my sister," Josselyn said, seeing the familiar look of pleading in her father's eyes. Even death did not erase his desire to protect his wife.

"We are proud, daughter," her father said, smiling gratefully. "You have made us proud."

"*Ago pugna quod intereo per veneration,*" Josselyn read aloud as her eyes lifted to the carved stone that graced the entryway to the hall. It seemed to flutter, appearing and disappearing in accordance with her desire to look at it.

"Yes, we have all lived with honor and this is our reward," her mother said. Laughter seemed to rise up around her, as both parents touched her arms, pulling her along with them to where the dining platform was raised. Music, low at first but growing with each heartbeat, filled the air. Servants appeared, as did people she knew from the surrounding village. They all smiled, as if welcoming her to them. The smell of roasted meat and sweet pastries became thick. This was a celebration—for her, welcoming her home.

CHAPTER 27

Evan pulled Josselyn's arm, dragging her body into his embrace as he struggled to stand. Her limbs flopped, uncontrolled, as he carried her across his quarters. Evan slammed his shoulder against the hand sensor, opening the door. His precarious hold on Josselyn began to slip, but he gripped tighter, hurrying through the corridors toward the medical unit.

Inside her, the cold nothingness he felt chilled him to the bone. His nose burned, but he refused to cry, to pity himself. Medical booths could not bring back the dead, but if he tried, if he could just get her there fast enough, maybe he could save her, maybe there was a bit of life inside her that he couldn't feel. And yet, a part of him had felt this moment, had felt her death long before it ever happened. He knew it would come and still he rushed to fight it.

Under the awkward set of her weight in his arms, his feet slipped, but he righted himself and continued on.

"What's happening?" Mei's voice rang down the corridor, reaching him before he could see her. "Who's stomping...? Evan?"

Evan met her dark eyes, his expression pleading in a way his words could not. "Mei, please, help."

"Jarek," Mei screamed, hurrying forward. "Evan, what happened? You shouldn't be carrying her. You're too weak. You can barely stand." And then Mei touched Josselyn, only to draw her hands back just as fast. "Evan? She's ice cold."

"No," Evan growled. "I just need to get her warm. Help me take her to the med—"

"What is it?" Jarek asked, running to join them.

"Josselyn's..." Mei took a step back, motioning to the unmoving form still clutched in Evan's arms.

Evan pushed past her, not wanting to hear anyone say she was lost to him as he carried Josselyn to the medical booth. He struggled to place her inside. Jarek was instantly there, helping him.

"Mei, start the medic," Jarek ordered.

"But she's gone. Look at her. She's turned blue. It's too late," Mei protested, even as she reached for the console.

"Just do it, Mei!" Evan barked. A violent shiver worked over him.

Mei pushed at the console screen. "This is what the wind told me. I thought it said we'd lose Parker. That he, as the new soul on this ship, would die."

"What are you talking about?" Jarek asked.

"Our son. I wanted his name changed because I didn't want to lose him. I didn't want fate to find him. We were docked on Werten and the desert wind said..." Mei paused, looking tragically at Evan. He felt her mix of pity for him and relief her son. "I'm sorry, Ev. Josselyn was the newest soul on this ship. I thought it meant Parker."

Evan had known Mei had her own premonitions of sorts. He'd known it shook her to the core and gripped her in fear over her son, but he hadn't pressed her for more information because, with his own power, he knew Parker would be fine. Bittersweet agony and relief flooded him—agony for his heart, relief for his friends and anger that he should have to choose between the two emotions. He blocked Mei and Jarek from his feelings. In that moment, as he stared at Josselyn's lifeless face, he knew the feelings in his heart as being his own. The love he felt was not just empathy for Josselyn, it wasn't just pity and sympathy. It was his. And that was the perfect irony—to finally discover completely and surely that what he felt was his alone, but to find such surety in his love's death.

"Start it again," Evan demanded when the unit made a low tone saying it was done. He heard Mei comply. The sound caused him to turn and he strode across the small room to the console to watch what she pushed. She was doing everything right, though her movements were too slow and shaky. "It won't kill your son to save her!" He pushed her roughly out of the way. Jarek caught his wife in his arms. "Have you ever considered that the wind on Werten lies? Or speaks a language unfamiliar to you? I've seen the great things Parker is set to do with his life. You will be grandparents several times over."

Mei gasped. "I was so sure."

"That is why you've been hiding yourself from me?" Jarek asked. "That is why you barely leave his side?"

Mei nodded, but Evan blocked her answer from his mind. Josselyn was not recovering. Part of him knew he would lose her, had seen her death, her pale face. Still, he was shocked by how much it hurt. Knowledge had not made it easier.

"I don't understand," Jarek said, drawing Evan from his thoughts. The booth kept trying to shut off to give a death report. "Zhang An said..."

"She said, '*If you do not recognize it, you will lose it*

and be forever alone'," Evan answered. He pushed the medical unit's console again and again to restart it, but each time the cycle became shorter and shorter until the display image froze with an error warning. Crossing to Josselyn, he stroked her cool cheek. "This is my fault. If I hadn't questioned what I felt for you as being empathy, I wouldn't have lost you."

"Evan, I'm sorry," Mei whispered.

"I'll have Rick change course for the Florencian moons. I can think of no better place to take her," Jarek said. "Viktor can make the appropriate ship logs. We will leave you alone with her."

"Don't bother to write it in the logs," Evan whispered, barely hearing his own words through the pain rolling over his soul. "There is no one to inform. She is the last of her people."

CHAPTER 28

JOSSELYN SMILED DOWN at her brothers, watching as they danced with pretty maids. Unlike life, in death they were not confined to the floor and many couples floated above the hall, twirling and laughing in merriment. Feeling a hand on her arm, she smiled as she glanced at her mother.

"Why don't you dance? Plenty of young knights and villein have no partner." Her mother motioned down to the lower tables to where a group of men sat laughing and drinking.

"I left someone behind," Josselyn said, as her mother gently stroked back her hair. "One of the men who saved me from the stone prison."

"You weren't awake all that long," Lady Craven put forth.

"No." Josselyn nodded. "But it was long enough."

"You were always so stubborn when it came to men." Lady Craven insisted. "Are you sure it wasn't just gratitude?"

"No. It was love." She closed her eyes, seeing Evan's face, hearing the whisper of his voice. "There was something when he touched me. I could sense him inside me and he felt me inside of him. I know now why I was so stubborn with men. It was because when I lived, he did not exist yet. My heart knew a hundred years ago that it belonged to Evan."

"If there was a way to make you forget him, would you take it?" Her mother stroked back her hair, like when she was a little girl. "Would you forget so that you may live here, with us, without regret?"

"No," Josselyn said. "But it's not regret I feel. I just miss him."

"Then you really do love him," her mother said, nodding. "It might not be too late."

"For what?"

"Your body is still intact. You can try to go back. We can try to help your spirit find its way, just like we helped you find your way to Jack."

Josselyn gasped, starting to smile, only to stop.

"Can you come with me? We can be a family again, live the life we should have lived."

"No, our bodies are long gone." Her mother leaned forward, kissing her cheek.

Suddenly, Josselyn frowned. She couldn't go back. What if she killed him? But maybe this time would be different. She knew her parents were all right and that their souls continued on in happiness. This time it could be different.

"What is it?" her mother asked.

"I don't know if he feels the same way." Josselyn took a deep breath. What if he couldn't grow to love her?

"If you love him..." Her mother glanced down to where her father talked to some of the knights. "Then you will take the chance. I did not raise you to have a closed heart and your father did not raise you to be scared of chances. If he does not love you, he is a fool. I know you're scared, my sweet child, but I will not have you live eternity with this regret. You should go and when you've lived a full life, a good life, you will come back to us and you will bring your heart with you. We will welcome you with open arms, and any you bring with you."

Josselyn closed her eyes briefly, as her mother kissed her again. When she opened them, her family was again around her. They were alone in the hall.

"We've waited a very long time for you. We can

wait longer," her father said. "Promise me you will live an honorable life, so we may be together when you do come back to us."

Josselyn nodded, tears rolling down her cheeks. She would miss her family, but parting from them wasn't like before. This time, she'd get a chance to say goodbye.

CHAPTER 29

Evan stared at Josselyn's face for so long the unmoving lines blurred and became a mass of pale colors. He knew when he finally blinked, he'd have to stand up. When he finally stood up, he'd have to take her from the medical booth. And when that happened, he would have to admit that it was over. Josselyn was dead.

He leaned against the far wall, ignoring the cold, hard metal along his back. When his dry eyes couldn't stay open, he blinked hard. Josselyn's face came back into focus. Finally, he pushed away from the wall. He took a step toward her and stopped. Without conscious reasoning, he went to the console and pressed the button, making the unit test her again. Inside, his heart squeezed. "Please, Josselyn, please." The unit beeped and he drew his hand away, knowing his actions to be futile. "Goodbye, Josselyn."

Evan grabbed his chest as a sharp pain radiated over him. He held onto the console for support. The ache was just like before and he realized that it was his suffering, not hers, that had been killing him. Knowing Josselyn, feeling her grief, so real and unsuppressed, made him find his. She awakened a deep part of his soul, a part of him he'd thought long dead. After his homeland was destroyed and his parents lost, he'd focused on taking care of his sister. After his sister died, he'd turned his attention to nursing Samantha back to health. By the time she recovered and they'd gathered the rest of the crew, he'd pushed a part of himself down deep. Josselyn didn't almost kill him with her past. It was his own emotional dam breaking which did it to him.

"*Aaah.*"

Evan's head snapped up, breathing hard. "Josselyn?"

"Evan."

Unable to believe what he was hearing, he looked at the console. A full scan ran, unlike before when it just shut off. His eyes wide, he looked at the booth. Josselyn blinked rapidly.

"Evan," she said again, this time louder. "Evan, are you there? I can't see you."

"I'm here." He pushed past his pain, forgetting

his sorrow as he went to her. Maybe he was dead. Maybe he was crazy. He didn't care either way. She was awake and she was calling his name. "I'm here."

"I thought I lost you," she whispered, gazing up at him. She didn't move within the booth and he saw the soft green light from the laser illuminating her face.

Evan gave a surprised laugh. "You thought *you* lost *me?*" He touched her face, tilting it fully towards him. "I lost you. You were dead."

"I know."

"Then how?" He ran his thumb over her lips, feeling her breath against the digit.

"My family helped me come back." Her eyes slowly focused on him, as if finally seeing him.

"For how long?" Evan leaned closer, almost too afraid to blink. He kept his voice soft. "I can't lose you again. Please stay with me." A hot tear streamed over his cheek. "I love you, Josselyn. Don't leave me again."

A shaking hand brushed the tear away. "Why would I leave? I came back for the chance of you."

Her eyes shone in a way that he'd never seen and when she smiled, he felt the light inside of her. There was hope and happiness and a tiny fear that had nothing to do with loss. And then warmth washed over him. Her love bathed him, filling him and giving him a peace unlike nothing he'd ever felt in his life. She didn't have to say the words. He heard her heart. It called to his.

"I don't want to hurt you," she said, the grain of fear inside her growing. "If my nearness causes you harm, I'll leave. I won't have another death on my hands."

"You didn't kill Jack. I did. I shot him. I knew you were dying, saw it in your future and I couldn't let you carry that burden."

"You knew I was dying and you came anyway? You killed Jack. You risked your life, your freedom. Why?"

"You do something to me, Josselyn." He touched his nose to hers lightly.

"I know, I make you forget yourself." She chuckled softly.

"No, you made me find myself." He craned his neck, unable to keep from kissing her. It was too hard to hold the position with her in the booth. "You won't hurt me with how you feel so don't hide from me. I was hurting myself. You saved me. I was hiding in a shell, too afraid to face memories because they were painful. The past built inside me and I kept pushing it down until finally it exploded."

"Get me out of here." Josselyn smiled and he basked in the expression. The stress around her eyes was gone. He'd never noticed it before but now that it was no longer marring her features, the brilliance of her moved him.

"Let the medical unit finish. I'm not risking you again." Evan smiled, content for the moment just to be with her.

"Evan? Who are you talking to?" Mei's voice broke into the spell between them. "I've come to bring you to your room. You've been in here for hours. Please, Evan. Come away."

"Never," he said.

"Hello, Mei," Josselyn said.

"What?" Mei gasped. Halted steps sounded behind him, but he didn't turn. "Blessed ancestors, how?"

"Love sometimes beats death," Josselyn answered. "And I love you, Evan."

"I'll tell the others." Mei still sounded stunned. "I'm, ah, glad you're all right."

Josselyn smiled, not looking away from him. Evan cupped her cheek, holding her the best he could. Joy flooded him. When they were alone, she said, "I didn't think it would be this easy."

"Easy?" He chuckled. "You were in stone for a hundred years. You came back from the dead. I wouldn't call that easy."

"I meant finding out if you returned my feelings. None of the rest matters." She touched his cheek. "Since I can't come out of this contraption and show my love for you properly, why don't you tell me how you found me? Violette's ship didn't detect that we were followed. How did you know?"

"We followed. The others knew you wouldn't trust them completely and with me sick, they thought it best for you to get another ride. Mei slipped a tracking device on you. I guess she said you two fought? Then Jarek led you to your family jewels so you could find them."

Her expression fell, as the green glow continued to cast her features. "You're pirates, aren't you?"

"We scavenge to make a living. Pirates are too confrontational. We tend to stay off other's radars when we can. Does that disappoint you?"

"Not as much as it should. How did they know I'd go for Jack?"

"That was the easy part. We all understand vengeance. We knew what you were going through. After Rick took you to the bar on the Zibi Fueling Docks, he paid Captain Violette for her services and for her silence. She took you to Rifflen." Evan told her everything in full detail.

Josselyn nodded, proceeding to tell him what happened to her—of Jack's words and deeds, of her mother's life and death. Tears swam in her gaze, but Evan knew she told him everything, even the painful. Then she told him of her death, of seeing her family, and he knew she believed that. He wanted to believe her, although death and life were such tricky things. Her idea of the afterlife gave hope and he didn't take that from her with his doubts.

"I have a sister. Jack and my mother," Josselyn finished.

"I know."

"How?" She arched a brow. The medical booth beeped and shut off.

Evan crossed to the console and pushed a couple buttons, looking over her results. She was perfectly healthy. "I believe the general sent Violette to pick you up. It was strange lucky that was who Rick found to take you to Rifflen. The general made her promise that when the time came for you to visit him, she would not interfere."

"Why would she?" Josselyn asked, pushing out of the medical unit to stand on her own. She crossed to him, her head tilted quizzically to the side.

"Violette is your sister."

"What?" Josselyn gasped. "We have to go back for her. We have to make sure she knows. If all you've said is true, then she might not know about me. She won't know why I came after her father. Please, Evan, I have to tell her. She's family."

"She swore revenge on you, Josselyn." He was amazed that she could so easily accept Jack's daughter as family, without hesitation. "You don't know her. She grew up as Jack's daughter. Let it go for now. Give her time. I felt her anger. It's too great a thing to face."

"How much time?"

"As much as these things take. First, I think we should go to Quazer. Violette gave me a disc key to a safe there. We should go and see what he left for you. Then the past can finally be over."

"It's already over," Josselyn said. "But I agree. I'll see what's in the safe, after..."

"After?" He grinned, feeling her desire feeding his own.

"After you ask me to no longer be your protected woman."

That took him by surprise. He tried to speak, but nothing came out.

"I'd much rather you ask me to be your wife."

Evan swept her into his arms, kissing her deeply. He still couldn't speak as emotions choked him. Walking brusquely down the corridor to his room, he took her to their quarters. Their lips didn't part as he laid her on the bed. Nothing needed to be said with words and Evan knew that this love he felt was his own and would last forever.

CHAPTER 30

Josselyn shivered, her body on fire. Part of her felt like this was a dream. The burden of her past left her and she was free. Someday, she'd see her family again and that gave her hope. Her only regret through all of it was Violette, but Evan was right. How could she go to her sister now? The woman would never believe anything she had to say.

"Don't," Evan whispered.

"What?" She arched her back as his lips trailed to her throat.

"Just give her time. Trust me. I know these things." Evan pulled back, smiling.

She adored that smile. Her mouth became dry and she swallowed hard at his meaningful look. Slowly, he tugged at her shirt, peeling it from her flesh. After pulling it over her head, he licked a trail between her breasts, stopping to kiss her nipples. Confident fingers reached for her waistband, tugging her pants until they slid down around her thighs. A low moan sounded in the back of his throat. Josselyn arched and his kisses slid down to her stomach and hips.

Evan kept pulling, kissing as he stripped her of the pants. "You're exquisite."

"Take your clothes off." She urged. Evan pushed up from the bed, easily stripping out of his shirt and pants. He stood naked, his eyes boldly on hers. The chocolate depths of his eyes bore into her, sweeping over her naked body.

Josselyn took in his naked form, the strong lines of his chest and arms, the trim tapering of his waist, his chiseled hips framing the full length of his erection. When he came forward, crawling like a stalking beast over her, she panted for breath. She saw the passion in him for her. It matched her own.

"Computer, dim lights," Evan said. Instantly, the room darkened, casting them in shadows. He was so handsome, with his tanned flesh thrown into heavy contrast. He didn't even have to touch her and her body lurched with desire.

His hand slid forward, pressing instantly to her heated center. The slick folds of her sex parted, damp and ready for him. With each pass of his fingers, moisture built to ease his way inside.

Josselyn tilted her head back, moaning. His delicate touch centered on the tight buds of nerves. She closed her eyes, arching her hips for more.

"Evan," she begged, maneuvering her legs along the outside of his. His arousal hit near her stomach. "Please."

Evan drew her body to his, slipping his shaft against her opening, branding her with his touch. She wrapped her legs around his waist, pulling him closer. Josselyn held onto his shoulders for support. Inside, she quivered and tensed.

His lips met hers, kissing gently as he entered her fully. Her muscles clenched, accepting him. Their soft moans intermingled and the intimate connection became dearer to her than anything else. Unhurriedly, he moved, taking his time as he made love to her. His finger found the sensitive nub guarding her entrance, circling it with fast strokes as he pushed her onward. The passion intensified between them, causing their pace to quicken. Suddenly, she could take no more. The tension built between them. Her toes curled as her legs fell to the side for leverage.

Evan lifted up on his hands, working harder. Josselyn's body racked with tremors as she met her release, crying out softly. His thrust became more powerful and urgent in his search for climax. Soon, his cry joined hers. He jerked almost violently, then held frozen for a moment before his head dropped down. Pulling out, he stretched next to her on the bed, holding her naked back against his chest.

"I never want to let you go," Evan said.

"Then, don't."

"This can be a hard life. When Gretori Zothos took my ship, he took all the money I had. I'm not a rich man. I can't buy you a home on some planet. This ship and this crew as my family is all I have to offer."

"Where would we go?" She turned in his arms to face him. "Both of our home worlds are dead. And I have plenty of money in gold and jewels in my castle. I know where it's all hidden, a place where you'd never even dream to look. All we have to do is fly back and get it."

"Are you sure it will be enough?"

"Are you going to ask me to marry you?" Josselyn giggled. "Because if you are, I've already said yes. I'm just waiting for your answer."

"I'll get Jarek." Evan pushed up from the bed.

"Jarek?" She was slower to get up, watching as he pulled on a pair of tight black pants.

"Law of the sky. As captain of this ship, he can marry us. If you're sure, I don't want to wait another second." Coming to her, he cupped her face. "I'm almost scared to leave you alone. Get dressed and come with me."

EVAN COULDN'T STOP SMILING as he looked at his bride. Josselyn wore one of his old shirts and a pair of pants and he'd never seen a more beautiful woman. The entire crew was there, standing in the commons as witnesses. Mei and her son sat in a chair. Dev and Jackson stood near the door, arms crossed. Rick smirked, his expression indicating he was on the verge of a joke. Viktor, Lucien and Lochlann merely grinned. All were happy to see Josselyn well.

Jarek wasn't exactly sure how to perform a marriage ceremony, so instead he improvised, keeping it short and to the point with two questions, 'Will you be his wife?' and 'Will you be her husband?'.

"Yes," they said in unison.

"Works for me. It's done," Jarek announced.

"Time to celebrate," Rick announced, lifting up a bottle of Earth whiskey. "Who's up for a drinking game?"

"Count us in," Lucien answered, tugging on his brother's arm.

"We must train," Dev said. Then to the newly-weds, he added, "Happy future."

"Dev," Jackson began.

"Jackson, we must train," Dev insisted.

"May you have a blessed marriage," Jackson said, following Dev out of the room.

"You guys have fun," Evan said.

"I am really happy for you," Mei said, holding her son and bouncing him lightly as she stood. Josselyn nodded at her. Theirs wasn't a deep friendship, but it was a start.

"Ah, come on, space cadet," Rick said. Evan noticed that Rick seemed to be back to his old self with the easy smiles and quick-witted jokes. "You're not going to turn into an old married man already, are you? It's only been five minutes."

"Enjoy your hand, Rick. I've got something much sweeter," Evan answered, sweeping his wife into his arms.

"Hand?" Josselyn wrapped her arms about his neck.

"Don't ask," Jarek answered.

"His girlfriend," Lucien said seconds later.

Evan saw the exact moment Josselyn got the meaning. She turned red, giggling into his shoulder.

"Ah, get you two off," Rick called. "We've plenty of time in space to test Josselyn's stamina at cards."

"I had three older brothers and a castle full of knights. I think I can hold my own," Josselyn answered as Evan carried her into the hall. Laughter followed them. Josselyn ran her fingers into Evan's short hair. "We could have stayed if you wanted to."

"No. Tonight I want you all to myself." He kissed the tip of her nose. "Later we'll celebrate this wedding properly when we can port somewhere befitting a lady."

"Mm, I can think of one place befitting a lady like me." She pressed her mouth to his as he came to their room, perfectly content to be in his arms. "And I'm already there."

CHAPTER 31

GLAMOUR DISTRICT, QUAZER, TWO MONTHS LATER...

"THE SECURITIES CENTER is right down this street." Josselyn smiled for her husband, despite the slight tightening in her stomach. She fingered the disc key snuggly rolled into the waistband of her skirt. The last few months with Evan had been perfect. She couldn't hide herself from him and she found, for the most part, she didn't mind how he sensed her moods. In many ways, it made him the perfect man. In a few ways, it made him irritating because he often sensed her moods before she was completely ready to face them.

"Did I tell you how beautiful you look today?" Evan asked, kissing her head.

Josselyn glanced down at the lightweight pink two-piece dress she wore. Shorter than the gowns she had growing up, its skirt moved with the breeze.

The tight bodice molded to her, forming a cocoon of hard material. Though gorgeous, it kept her from feeling Evan's hands pressing into her sides when he touched her.

"Do you think Violette will be here?" she asked, again glancing around.

"The guys didn't see her ship and it's a hard one to miss. Lucien accessed the logs and she wasn't registered. I think Rick's erratic maneuvering through deep space lost their ship." Evan slipped his arm around her shoulders as they walked.

The white streets shimmered in the bright sunlight as a tropical breeze filtered through the Glamour District. A planet completely dedicated to luxury and the rich, Quazer even had docking fees, security fees and a long list of other fees designed to ensure only those who could afford to be there actually landed. Smooth stone arches with crystal insets lined the sidewalks, creating colorful streaks of light on the ground.

"Besides," Evan nodded to the side, "we've got plenty of backup."

Josselyn saw a flash of Viktor and Lucien asking for directions from a local worker. On the other side, Mei and Jarek walked arm in arm. Further down the street, Jackson and Lochlann flirted with a group of women in formal silk gowns. Dev stayed on the ship, even though all manner of humanoids were welcome. The only person she didn't see was Rick, but everyone had assured her they would be watching every step.

The securities building glistened like all the other shops. Laser protection bars striped the windows and encrusted silver lined the intricately carved signs. Josselyn imagined that this place looked like a gathering of nobles, rich and famous from around the galaxy. Their demeanor and actions spoke of money and power.

Inside the securities building, Josselyn and Evan were met with gracious smiles. Saleswomen tried to beckon them to their counters by waving their arms over alluring rows of precious stones and minerals. For the not-so-human humanoids, there were jars of red slime and purple goo. A couple of pale yellow-skinned ladies used them to decorate their arms, the slime creating a chemical reaction with their flesh, making it bubble up in jewelry-like patterns.

"I wish to open a safe," Josselyn said to a saleslady.

The woman's jet-black hair wound high above her head in a large spiraling pattern, shaping into a cone. Small blue flecks decorated the hairstyle, centering around a blue disc.

Josselyn reached beneath the edge of the hard bodice to the rolled waistband. Tugging the material, she let the disc key drop into her palm. "I have a key."

The woman glanced down at the disc key and her smile faltered some. "Of course, madam, you will please follow me."

Josselyn took Evan's arm, clutching it for support. The woman led them past all the displays toward a large oval protruding from the wall. They stepped over the ledge, walking into what looked to be wall. Instead, they passed through like air into a long, oval hallway with a flat, narrow strip of floor to stay level. A small platform screen on a long circular column sat at the end. Pulling the blue disc from her hair, she pressed it to the screen. It dangled on the end of a long, straight pin. After it scanned, she pushed the pin back into her hairstyle and turned to Josselyn.

"Place your disc on the screen and enter the code. When you are finished, remove the disc." The woman nodded once at Evan and left.

"Code?" Josselyn frowned. "Did you know there was a code?"

"No," Evan said. "Put the disc down and see what happens."

"The others can't see us in here."

"This has to be one of the most secure facilities on the planet. I think we'll be all right." Evan nodded toward the screen.

Josselyn pressed the disc key inside the center ring. The gel inside the screen molded around it and held the disc inside. Over it, a delicately scrolled question appeared on the screen in black, "How should you live and die?"

"With honor," Josselyn said. "*Ago pugna quod intereo per veneration.*"

A light whoosh sounded behind them and she turned to find a long table crossing the walkway, blocking the exit and held up on each end by the sides of the oval wall. Several small contents lay out on the table, including a holo-box and a soft, black bag. It was shinier than the one found on the ship, but just as old.

"What are all these things?" Josselyn asked, not recognizing any of the technological items.

Evan touched a thin square. An image of Josselyn's face appeared in holographic perfection. The name Josse Lynne Stephans appeared beneath it with a number. "They're identification papers and a planetary ID number. Some of it is blank, like birth date and age, but Viktor can fill it in for you." Evan pointed at a few other items. "These are official birth records, a credit disc for money. Josselyn, this is a complete new identity. Jack gave you a means to hide."

"You mean to cover up what he and the Federation had done." She didn't take them.

"Perhaps, but these documents are hard to forge." Evan pushed the birth record.

"Daughter of Federation General Jack Stephans," Josselyn read. She nearly gagged. "I don't want this. I don't want anything of his."

"We can't leave it here." Evan picked it up and put it into his pocket. "We'll take it back to the ship and then you can decide. I have a feeling it might be useful."

"Fine." Josselyn wasn't happy with the idea, but her anger would have been misguided if she turned it on Evan. Jack was who she really was irritated with. Tapping her finger on the holo-box, she drew her hand back and laced it through her husband's arm. An image of Jack appeared. He looked to be in his late forties and wore the shiny white she'd come to associate with him.

"Josselyn, I'm glad you are well." Jack's image said. "It's what I've hoped for these last, long years. By this time and because you are still alive after the term of your imprisonment has ended, we have probably spoken. Knowing the temperament of your family, we have not spoken kindly. So much has happened and changed since that day long ago and I must force myself to remember that you don't know the good I've tried to do. All you know are my sins. I cannot take back that which was done, but I can give you a new life. With these papers, you will never have to explain your age or your past. As my daughter, a general's daughter, you will have the freedom to pass by Federation ports unhampered. I cannot leave the life I have chosen. The Federation has granted me the home, which I so longed to be a part of in those years you knew me, as a reward for my services. I know it is not the land it once was, but all it is, I give to you."

Josselyn held on to Evan as Jack continued to tell her how to use her space credits and the identification papers. One of the items was a key to a personal ship with navigational guides to help her fly it. On the ship, she'd find clothing and a machine to download knowledge into her brain to help her function in the new time. He'd thought of everything, even supplied her with a list of possible new home worlds and directions to them, should she decide to relocate. He even offered to let her live with him, though he knew she'd never take him up on it.

"If I am dead, I hope it was in atonement of my sins and that you will be able to forgive me now. I am truly sorry, Josselyn. All I ever wanted was to be a part of what you had. I never meant to destroy that which I loved so dearly." Jack's image sighed and he nodded once before the holo-box turned off.

"He must have sent this when he didn't hear back from your pardon," Evan said, "after they freed your mother from stone. He knew he could save you after you defrosted, but didn't know about the prisoners being crushed."

"I know he says he tried to atone for what happened, but I don't know if I'll ever forgive him." Josselyn looked up at her husband. "Does that make me a bad person?"

"No, starbeam, it makes you an honest person." He kissed her temple and she began gathering the safe's contents, putting them into the black handbag. "Jarek has arranged lodgings for a few nights to get us all off the ship. It's not often we get a spa holiday and since we've already paid for the landing, we might as well enjoy ourselves."

Josselyn fingered the black bag as Evan pressed the disc key molded into the screen. Slowly, it was released and he handed it to his wife.

"With Quazer's security, no one's getting out of the docks with weapons. We'll be safe here even if your sister finds us. I'm suddenly having the feeling that she might. She knows we'll eventually come here if we want to open the safe."

"Maybe Jack's present will have some use after all," Josselyn mused. "If Violette comes, it might be the only way of convincing her that what happened was just."

IF JOSSELYN DIDN'T THINK her husband had talents, seeing Captain Violette waiting for her outside the securities building would have made her a true believer. Steely green eyes, eerily reminding her of Jack, pierced her. Josselyn had been sick on Violette's ship, but now she could see the family resemblance in the woman. Violette had their mother's cheekbones and chin, though her demeanor and facial expressions were all Jack.

"I'm going to her." Josselyn clutched the black bag. "I don't want to spend our life together looking over my shoulder, waiting for her to run me through."

Violette's eyes narrowed as Josselyn approached and it was clear by the woman's expression that she didn't expect Josselyn to be so forward. The captain's gaze shifted around the crowded street before settling over Josselyn's shoulder. Evan would not have left them alone and assuredly followed behind.

"You're braver than I thought," Violette said. "Or stupider."

"I won't speak ill of your father to you, but the man you knew is not the Jack I did." Josselyn stopped, keeping distance between them, happy to have the crowd around and hoping that would be enough to keep Violette from attacking. She wasn't worried about anything the woman would do to her, but she would hate to see her sister hurt.

"I think I knew him much better than you." Violette set her jaw, her eyes narrowing. There was so much anger and hate inside her.

"Before your mother—" Josselyn began.

"My mother died when I was born."

"Before she married Jack, she was my mother." Josselyn didn't move, didn't take her eyes off her sister's.

"Is that what this is? Mommy left you and so you sought revenge on the man who won her heart?" Violette snorted.

Josselyn didn't want to be the one to tell the woman that their mother could never love Jack or that she married him out of depression and desperation. No child should have to hear they were conceived out of fear and convenience.

Josselyn reached into the black bag and found the holo-box. "You are my sister and I don't wish you any harm. Long ago, when your father was a young man, he knew me and was protected by my father, Lord Craven. We grew up together in my castle home on Florencia's fifth moon. Jack betrayed us and was part of the invasion that took our homes, our lives and imprisoned me in stone. I'm sure your father was not the same man, but he knew he had to pay for his past sins. Because of him, thousands of our people died, your mother's people."

"My father was a humanitarian. Because of him millions lived," Violette spat. "My mother was a lady, a fine lady he saved. I did not interfere before because I promised him I wouldn't, but that promise is fulfilled and I will not stop until you pay for what you have done."

"I didn't expect you to believe me, but before you ruin your life chasing revenge and trying to get to me, watch this." Josselyn tossed the holo-box at her sister. "Perhaps your father's words will convince you to find a better path."

Josselyn backed away, keeping her eyes on Violette's. A hand slipped onto her arm and she instinctively knew it was Evan. As they walked cautiously away, Josselyn glanced over her shoulder. The uncertainty of the future didn't frighten her. She had Evan and the rest of the crew as her new family and she had the knowledge of what was to come after death. Violette had slipped into the crowd and disappeared. Lochlann and Jackson materialized a second later. Jackson nodded at her and they moved to follow Violette.

"Will she come for me?" Josselyn asked.

"It's hard to tell. There's too much anger and confusion. But she doesn't strike me as an impatient woman. She will not act rashly and she will not act today." He spoke with such certainty that she didn't question him. "Let's find that hotel. I can't wait to get you alone and out of that impossible shirt."

"Have I told you how much I love you today, husband?" she asked, resting her head against his shoulder.

"No, but I felt it the second I woke up." Evan held her close as they walked down the glittering street. "And I hope to feel it every day of our long lives together."

"Long?" Josselyn arched a brow.

"Mm, very long." Evan laughed.

"And what did you see in this long life?"

"Happiness, starshine, complete and utter happiness." Evan swung her around, meeting his mouth to hers.

CHAPTER 32

EPILOGUE

Rick slipped into his chair at the gaming table in the commons. "So, which element is she? Earth because of the prison statue she was trapped in like stone?"

"I thought you didn't care," Lochlann answered, stealing a piece of fruit off Viktor's trencher of food.

"Hey," Viktor protested, slapping at him. "Get your own."

"I don't, just curious," Rick said, reaching to grab his own piece while Viktor was distracted.

"I think she's water because we found her on and ice planet," Jackson said.

"Air," Viktor said, "because she died and became a spirit."

"All I know is she's not metal. I'm metal." Rick

hit his chest. "Hard as steel."

Coming around the corner, Evan grinned. "I don't know what element she is. All I know is that she's mine."

"Eh!" Viktor threw a piece of sliced fruit at Evan's head. "Out of here! This party is for bachelors."

"That doesn't help the rest of them." Rick chuckled.

"Them?" Jackson asked. "The last time I checked, you were as cursed as the rest of us."

"Not worried," Rick said. "I already told you, I'm metal and so will my soul mate be, just as soon as I steal her pleasure droid body from the nearest brothel."

"I hope she electrocutes your bal—" Lochlann began.

"Oh, not right!" Rick jumped slightly in his seat. "Don't pout because you're jealous of me."

"Seriously, Ev," Viktor said. "Which element do you think she is?"

"Sorry, space cadets," Evan popped the fruit Viktor had thrown at him into his mouth. "I really don't know. Guess you'll have to figure that one out for yourselves."

The End

THE SERIES CONTINUES...

Space Lords Series
His Frost Maiden
His Fire Maiden
His Metal Maiden
His Earth Maiden
His Woodland Maiden

HIS FIRE MAIDEN

A Space Lords Novel

Dev has found a home with a misfit outlaw band of space pirates and he will do anything to protect his makeshift family. He knows he will never be accepted into human society. The demonic race of his birth shuns him and the humans fear him. So when the woman of his dreams comes gunning for his crew, the fiery maiden leaves him no choice but to show just how naughty his demon can be.

Prologue Excerpt

Rifflen Federation Military Base, Desert Planet of Rifflen, V Quadrant

Violette Craven Stephans stared as the blood

trailed down her forearm over her hand, only to watch as it drip steadily from her fingertips onto the hard tile floor by her feet. For a long moment the deliberate cut didn't even hurt, but then a deep pain radiated over her, and she cried out as she moved to pull the limb close to her body in a protective gesture.

"This is a blood oath, Violette, between us." Her father grabbed her wrist and shook it hard, forcing her eyes to meet his steely green ones. His fingers slipped in her blood as he held too tight. "I need you to remember this moment. I need you to remember what I tell you. And I need you never to speak of it to anyone."

Violette was still too stunned by the fact that her father had actually cut her to give him a quick answer. In all of her eight years, she had never seen her father angry with her, let alone violent enough to do her harm. What made it all the more puzzling is that she hadn't been doing anything wrong—at least, she didn't think she had been. It wasn't like the time she had burrowed a tiny hole in the military base's transparent exterior wall because she wanted some sand from outside. The entire military structure was located beneath the moving white dunes of Rifflen's sandy surface. That one hole caused a pressure crack that could have caved in and buried the four hundred and sixteen residents of the base. For that she'd been stuck in room seclusion for a mere two days.

"Your blood is mine, and mine is yours," he continued. "Do you understand? If you do not honor your word, nothing in your life will matter for you will have forsaken your blood. Do you understand me? Blood is everything."

Her father, General Jack Stephans, was an important man—not just because he was her father, a general in the Federation Military, and the sole authority on the Rifflen base, but because he was a humanitarian and an alienitarian. He dedicated much of his life to promoting equality and fairness between alien races.

"The universes are a big place," he would tell people. *"Large enough to hold all species. Humanoids are no better than a Kintok, or a Torg, or a…"*

"Do you understand?" he repeated, louder than before, shaking her from her scattered thoughts. The smell of liquor was thick on his breath.

She looked from his eyes to her blood and then back again, trying to reconcile what she knew with what had just happened. Frightened, she nodded. The fear she felt of him at that moment outweighed the physical pain caused by his thin blade. Her fingers tingled with numbness. In truth, she didn't understand. "I only wanted to watch the new holobox. It didn't say it was military access only. It didn't need a code to view it. I thought it would be one of your species profiles or an award invitation. You always let me see them."

The holo-box was a standard issue Federation communication device, initially used to send encoded memos and official orders. Now, they were utilized by the military for all sorts of formal letters, when more than a voice was needed. Private messages were always encrypted so that the wrong person couldn't watch them.

Instead of an award, the holographic recording had shown the small image of her father, standing in his shiny white uniform on the round disc on top of the box. It appeared as if it had been recorded that very morning. He'd been talking about some strange things too, things that didn't make any sense to her adolescent brain.

"Josselyn, I'm glad you are well," the recording had said. *"It's what I've hoped for these last, long years. By this time and because you are still alive after the term of your imprisonment has ended, we have probably spoken. Knowing the temperament of your family, we have not spoken kindly. So much has happened and changed since that day long ago, and I have to force myself to remember that you don't know the good I've tried to do. All you know is my sins. I cannot take back that which was done, but I can give you a new life. With these papers, you will never have to explain your age or your past. As my daughter, a general's daughter, you will have*

the freedom to pass by Federation ports unhampered. I cannot leave the life I have chosen. The Federation has granted me the home, which I so longed to be a part of in those years you knew me as a reward for my services. I know it is not the land it once was, but all it is, I give to you."

Her father looked at his desk and frowned. His grip on her arm loosened, and she pulled her wrist free. She took a slow step back, careful not to make too many sudden movements. Her eyes darted to the thick oak door of her father's private office. The wood seemed out of place in the metal construct of the military base. Carved patterns spoke of crafts-manship and time, not portability and ease of assembly. A barren fireplace graced one wall, surrounded by emblems and even a banner with the Craven family crest. Craven had been her mother's title and name, a title her father had taken when they married, a title that would be passed on to her —the *only* child of the couple. Her mother had died soon after she was born. All Violette had were the memories and descriptions her father had given her. That title was her gift from her mother. The name, a few holographic images, a notion, and a family crest—that was Violette's mother's legacy. How could her father think to give any Craven land to this Josselyn woman?

Violette's legs trembled, as she was unsure what to make of her father's expression. His shortly cropped black-gray hair and hard green eyes appeared both menacing and familiar. He wore his white, long tunic uniform, material that gleamed as it reflected the soft orange firelight. A thin brown stripe ran down the sides of his legs and arms, signifying his rank. Her clothing mimicked his in style though the loose pants and tunic were blue and cut with shorter sleeves.

"Who is Josselyn? Why did you call her your daughter?" Her eyes filled with tears. Violette didn't have siblings. "I don't understand. Why would you give her your land? I'm your daughter. Me! My mother died after giving birth to me. You said—"

"There are things you cannot understand," he whispered. "Things you cannot comprehend. The land I spoke of does not belong to you. You will never see it." Then louder, his eyes clearing as he found her inching away from him in fear, he added, "You *must* promise me you will not say a word about what you have seen, and promise that you will not interfere in this matter because—"

"Who is she?" Violette demanded, dying to discover the answer. She had never seen his eyes so cold.

"There are things you don't understand, Violette!" Then, softening his demeanor, as if the gesture took great effort on his part, he continued, "You are my daughter. My blood daughter. As my heir, you will be well taken care of. The land I speak of is not for you. You would not want it. All that you see here is yours, including what is in my safe. Always remember that this base operates on the old code, and you will not be questioned, or stopped from taking what is yours. You will always be provided for. I have seen to it."

"I remember the old code," she said softly. "I won't forget."

"Good girl." He gave her a small nod. "That is why this oath is important because I know you will not be able to break your word to me. Someday, a woman named Josselyn might attempt to find me. She's my history, my personal ghost, and she's a furious one. You must not get in her way. Whatever she comes to do, you must promise me you will not try to stop her. What will come is what must be, for events were put into motion long before you were born."

Her father rolled the sleeve of his shiny, pristine uniform and reached for his knife, holding it gingerly in his palm.

"What else did the holo-box say? You didn't let it finish," she interrupted what he was doing. She pulled her bleeding arm closer to her stomach. The blood wet her shirt, but she didn't care.

His eyes moved briefly to where the holo-box sat on his desk next to a stack of ID chips, intergalactic maps, and official travel papers. When he again looked at her, he'd banished the anger from his grave expression. "Promise me that when Josselyn comes, you will not interfere. Someday you will be a great captain, heir to my fortune and to my position on this base should you choose that path. But, blood is thicker than military ranking. Promise me, when Josselyn comes, you will obey my wishes and not lift a finger to stop what she chooses to do. You will let events play out as they are meant to regardless of the cost."

"I don't understand," Violette protested, puzzled. Her father lifted his knife and sliced through his arm. Without giving her a choice, he lunged forward and grabbed her, placing her cut to his to bind the wounds together. Their blood mingled on her skin, and she felt dizzy. The acrid odor seemed all at once overwhelming and comforting.

"Your blood has made the oath for you. The scar you are left with will remind you of the promise, but I would have you say the words. Say you promise. You will not ask about Josselyn again. You will not speak of my history unless I speak of her first. And, when the time comes, if I ask you to do something, to help her, you will do what I say without question and without hesitance. Do you understand me? Say you promise."

"I promise." Violette nodded, and her father released her arm.

"Good girl. Good." He suddenly seemed despondent. The general stood for a long moment, staring at his wound. "I am sorry you looked at the box, Violette, thus making this necessary. I wished for you never to have known."

She backed away from him, wanting nothing more than to run to the furthest corner of the military base. There was no escaping the enclosed building beneath the moving white sands, but she knew every secret hiding spot, every tight corner.

Her father turned from her and lifted a decanter to pour himself a drink. "Before you go to your virtual flying lesson see the medic and have your cut attended to, but leave the scar. I will not have you forgetting your promise."

For a complete, up-to-date booklist, visit
www.MichellePillow.com

ABOUT MICHELLE M. PILLOW

New York Times & *USA TODAY* Bestselling Author

Michelle loves to travel and try new things, whether it's a paranormal investigation of an old Vaudeville Theatre or climbing Mayan temples in Belize. She believes life is an adventure fueled by copious amounts of coffee.

Newly relocated to the American South, Michelle is involved in various film and documentary projects with her talented director husband. She is mom to a fantastic artist. And she's managed by a dog and cat who make sure she's meeting her deadlines.

For the most part she can be found wearing pajama pants and working in her office. There may or may not be dancing. It's all part of the creative process.

Come say hello! Michelle loves talking with readers on social media!

www.MichellePillow.com

facebook.com/AuthorMichellePillow

twitter.com/michellepillow

instagram.com/michellempillow

bookbub.com/authors/michelle-m-pillow

goodreads.com/Michelle_Pillow

amazon.com/author/michellepillow

youtube.com/michellepillow

pinterest.com/michellepillow

COMPLIMENTARY EXCERPTS
TRY BEFORE YOU BUY!

Rebellious Prince
by Michelle M. Pillow

A Modern Day Dragon Lords World Story

Cat-shifter Prince Rafe knows that technically he's supposed to be going to Earth to find a bride, but he doesn't see the need to rush things. While his dragon-shifter neighbors appear all too eager to claim their mates and settle down, he's all for putting that final moment off and enjoying his little trips through the portal. Yeah, yeah, eventually he'll have to marry and set a good example for his people because on his planet females are rare and they need to have children and blah blah blah. But honestly, cat-shifters are known to embrace their feral side and it would take a very impressive female to tame his.

Then he sees Jenna Kearney and all bets are off.

For release information visit www.
MichellePillow.com

THE SAVAGE KING
CAT-SHIFTER ROMANCE

The Savage King by Michelle M. Pillow

Read about Captain Jarek's cat-shifting brothers!

Lords of the Var® Book One by Michelle M. Pillow

Bestselling Cat-shifter Romance Series

Cat-shifting King Kirill knows he must do his duty by his people. When his father unexpectedly dies, it's his destiny to take the throne and all of the responsibility that entails. What he hadn't prepared for is the troublesome prisoner that's now his to deal with.

Undercover Agent Ulyssa is no man's captive. Trapped in a primitive forest awaiting pickup, she's going to make the best out of a bad situation...

which doesn't include falling for the seductions of a king.

About *Lords of the Var®* (Books 1-5)

You met their father, King Attor, in Dragon Lords Books 1-4, now meet the Var Princes!

The cat-shifter princes were raised to not believe in love, especially love for one woman, and they will do everything in their power to live up to their father's expectations. Oh, how the mighty will fall.

The Savage King Excerpt

Kirill watched the door to his bedroom open. He'd been sitting in the dark, trying to relieve the stress headache that had built behind his eyes for the last week. The pain started at the base of his skull and radiated up to his temples until he could hardly see straight.

A heavy responsibility had been thrust on his shoulders, a responsibility he really hadn't prepared himself for, the welfare of the Var people. King Attor had not left him in a good position. He'd rallied the people to the brink of war, convinced them that the Draig were their enemy, and even went so far as to attack the Draig royal family.

Kirill wanted to see peace in the land. However, he knew the facts didn't bode well for it. The Draig had a long list of grievances against King Attor and the Var kingdom.

Before his death, the king had ordered an attack on the four Draig princes, all of which ended horribly for the Var. The worst was when Prince Yusef was stabbed in the back, a most cowardly embarrassment for the Var guard who did it. If he hadn't been executed in the Draig prisons, he would've been ostracized from the Var community. Luckily, Prince Yusef survived or they'd already be at battle.

Attor had also arranged for the kidnapping of Yusef's new bride. The Draig Princess Olena had been rescued, or that too would've led to war. The old king had even tried to poison Princess Morrigan, the future Draig queen, on two separate occasions. She too lived. And those were only a few of the offenses Kirill knew about in the few weeks before King Attor's death. He could just imagine what he didn't know.

Kirill sighed, feeling very tired. He'd known since birth that the day would come when he'd be expected to step up and lead the Var as their new king. He just hadn't expected it to be for another hundred or so years. His father had been a hard man, whom he'd foolishly believed was invincible.

"Here kitty, kitty, kitty." His lovely houseguest's whisper drew his complete attention from his heavy thoughts.

Ulyssa bent over like she expected him to answer to the insulting call. He dropped his fingers from his temple into his lap, and a quizzical smile came to his lips. As he watched her, he wasn't sure if he was angered or amused by her words.

"Are you in here, you little furball?" she said, a little louder.

She wore his clothes. Never had the outfit looked sexier. His jaw tightened in masculine inter-est, as he unabashedly looked her over. All too well did he remember the softness of her body against his and the gentle, offering pleasure of her sweet lips. She'd made soft whimpering noises when he'd touched her, yielding, purring sounds in the back of her throat. Even with the aid of nef, he was surprised by how easily and confidently she melted into him. The Var were wild, passionate people and were drawn to the same qualities in others. He suspected she'd be an untamed lover.

Too bad she'd belonged to his father first. In his mind, that made her completely untouchable though none would dare question his claim if he were to take her to his bed. Technically, by Var law, she belonged to him until he chose to release her. For an insane moment, he thought about keeping her as a lover. He knew he wouldn't, but the thought was entertaining.

Kirill's grin deepened. Ulyssa strode across his home to the bathroom door with an irritated scowl. It was obvious she didn't see him in the darkened corner, watching her. He detected her engaging smell from across the room, the smell of a woman's desire. It stirred his blood, making his limbs heavy with arousal. And, for the first time since his father's death, his headache relieved itself.

"Hum, maybe I'm looking too high. I'm sure there has to be a little cat door here somewhere. Come here, little kitty. Where are you hiding?"

His slight smile fell at her words. It was easy to detect her mocking tone.

"Where's your little kitty door, huh?" Ulyssa whispered to herself, her blue gaze searching around in the dark.

Kirill grimaced in further displeasure. He watched her open the door to his weapons cabinet. Her eyes rounded, and he thought she might take one. She didn't. Instead, she nodded in appreciation before closing the door and continuing her search for an exit.

She stopped at a narrow window by his kitchen

doorway. Her neck craned to the side, as she tried to see out over the distance. Kirill knew she looked at the forest. From under her breath, he heard her vehement whisper, "Where exactly did you little fur balls bring me? Ugh, I need to get out of this flea trap, even if I have to fight every one of you cowardly felines to do it. I've fought species twice as big and three times as frightening. A couple of little kitty cats don't scare me."

If this insolent woman wanted to play tough, oh, he'd play. Curling gracefully forward, Kirill shifted before his hands even touched the ground. He let one thick paw land silently on the floor, followed by a second. Short black fur rippled over his tanned flesh, blending him into the shadows. His clothes fell from his body, and he lowered his head as he crept forward. A low sound of warning started in the back of his throat. He was livid.

Buy The Savage King

To find out more about Michelle's books visit www.MichellePillow.com

PLEASE LEAVE A REVIEW

THANK YOU FOR READING!

Please take a moment to share your thoughts by leaving a review.

Be sure to check out Michelle's other titles at

www.michellepillow.com